PRAISE FOR

MACOVEN

"This is Doc Jacobs' second book, and it could not be more different than the first. This latest offering is exemplary of the definition of fiction, 'one of the most popular genres of literature, a story featuring imaginary characters and events.' *MaCoven* will hold your interest until the last paragraph, which will sum up the journey through Purgatory, or will it?"

—Bill Sheehan, Author of *Together We Served* and *A Tail Among Tales*

"I'm so incredibly honored and privileged to be able to have read and remark on this incredible work of art that was written by a hero in many facets—whom I can call a friend. Before MaCoven, Doc Jacobs was able to translate his stories from the battlefield and beyond into an inspirational journey of resilience and determination in There and Back Again: Stories from a Combat Navy Corpsman. But MaCoven doesn't translate anything. It creates space to take us on an incredible journey of what it could be like, finding ourselves in a world where we're able to tap into the powers of creating justice with dark magic. Doc took me on an adventure that was thrillingly unexpected, and a joy to read. MaCoven shows an incredible imagination and skillset that Doc has hiding away with his many other talents, one that I'm looking to see more of.

"[To Doc:] Your hard work and dedication to your craft is evident in this piece of work. I wish I could say I'm surprised at how fantastic this read was, but I wouldn't expect anything less of you."

—Robert Graves, USMC, Author of *How to Grow a Beard: A Military Guide Back into Civilian Life, Creator* and Host of the #YearOfTheVet Podcast

MaCoven
by Doc Jacobs

© Copyright 2023 Doc Jacobs

ISBN 978-1-64663-820-8

Published by

 köehlerbooks™

3705 Shore Drive
Virginia Beach, VA 23455
800-435-4811
www.koehlerbooks.com

MAC☾VEN

DOC JACOBS

VIRGINIA BEACH
CAPE CHARLES

PROLOGUE

John startled awake to a sound like radio static filling the heavy dark air.

What the fuck? Why am I stuck to this hot chair? I hate being hot, and this is not—wait, who the fuck is doing this? John screamed in his head. *I don't remember even being in a position where someone could have kidnapped me. Maybe it's those assholes from the firm across town. Scumbag dumb fucks! They'll pay for this!*

John took a deep breath and then yelled out. "Stan! I swear to everything holy, if you're behind this, I'll rip your testicles out and feed them to your family in meatball subs!"

"Shut up and watch the screen! *Your* show is about to begin," commanded a voice from a loud surround sound system that was heavy on the bass.

John paused momentarily, trying to see if he recognized the voice but found himself admiring the sound system.

The screen in front of him flickered to life and began to show early memories of John as if he were watching a movie of his life.

What the hell? Who would have these videos? I don't even think my mom and dad videoed some of these moments, he thought with a head tilt.

Perplexed, he sat silently watching his life play out on the screen.

I thought your life flashing before your eyes only happened when you died, but I don't think I'm dead. I'm feeling everything. Speaking of which, why is it getting hotter in here? This metal chair feels hotter too. He tried to struggle but couldn't budge his bonds. He couldn't take his eyes off the screen.

"Wait, why is this speeding up? You're skipping through some of the really good stuff!" John yelled as he tried to pull his head away from the screen but couldn't.

Though John protested the speeding up of the film through what he thought were good moments in his life, the film sped up even more.

The film flipped through years rapidly and suddenly stopped on a snowy morning at a coffee shop.

"Wait, why is this meaningful? I'm just getting coffee for me and my clients here! What is the significance?" John demanded but felt forced to watch.

"Wait! This is the guy?"

John heard a different voice over the booming sound system before everything cut to darkness.

CHAPTER ONE

The morning was a typical start to a snowy day in Portland, Oregon. The winds blew from the northeast, which usually made for a long day of cold heavy snow. Although the storm was still light, it was forecasted to pick up over the later morning hours. The city began to come to life.

Maddie began to layer up as she sat on the wooden bench just inside the apartment building's front door. *Ugh! Why does Mom make me put these bread bags on over my socks? The bags aren't even the same brand,* she thought as she slipped into her aging snow boots. *At least this poofy jacket matches the rest of everything and is still fluffy enough to keep me warm.* She trekked to the thin glass door with her backpack on and her scarf tied snuggly. *What is this door even blocking? It sure isn't the wind.*

By the time she got to the apartment building's front door, her insulated gloves had just covered her fingers. She pushed the cold handle to open the door and head into the snowfall.

Maddie didn't mind this walk to school, regardless of the weather. *I think it's crazy how even at our age, we still see the typical school cliques all around. Even with the snowfall and being bundled up, I can see the nerds swapping their new animated trading cards and talking about the latest sci-fi movie.*

She trudged through the wind and snow behind them. She stayed close enough to hear their chatter and banter about their favorite characters and the villains but far enough away not to get roped into the group or the conversation.

I have heard these kids talk about this movie for weeks now. Aw man, these nerds and their trading cards! If I have to listen to this stupid discussion about which character is best one more time, I'm going to lose it. Still, I guess it's better than hearing about the latest fashion trends and which boy is the cutest, she thought as she eyed the group of girls giggling together ahead of the nerds. This was her third straight day following these same groups to school.

This morning, she noticed a light-blue foreign-made sporty sedan speeding through the neighborhood. The sedan driver, seemingly inconvenienced by the approaching stop sign, barely slowed down. He did so just as some elementary school children, bundled up with their heads down and focused on finding their footing off the curb, were about to cross the street in the crosswalk.

The sound of the vehicle's horn lasted longer than the driver's time on the brake pedal. The driver barely slowed down or swerved and unknowingly hit a pothole filled with the cold sludge of rain and snow from the night before. A wall of freezing muck spewed onto the children.

This wasn't this driver's first time through the neighborhood. Maddie had noticed this individual many times driving recklessly through the residential streets. She had seen him barely slow down near stop signs while reaching for something in the passenger seat, being consumed by his mobile device, suddenly stopping, erratically swerving off the road, making illegal U-turns, and other countless reckless maneuvers. But this one pissed off Maddie the most.

How is it that people get away with this shit? Why aren't there any consequences for people like that?

She was not pleased one bit about this. Maddie had never been one to jump the gun and had always been thorough about every decision in her life. This day, however, she wanted to do something different and decided to go get some hot cocoa from a local coffee shop. This little treat for herself always helped calm her down.

She took her usual route through the neighborhood, but as she neared the school, she took a left instead of her usual right. She kept heading on that road into the incorporated area. As she neared the bigger business buildings, she noticed many coffee shops, gas stations, and fast-food restaurants.

She gasped angrily when she turned the corner of a large corporate building.

"You have got to be kidding me!" she yelled out.

There, in a handicapped spot in front of the coffee shop, sat the light-blue sedan. Maddie looked for a handicapped placard or license plate on the car but didn't see one.

She walked up to a van idling nearby, clearly waiting on the parking spot, and signaled the driver to roll their window down.

"How long have you been waiting here?" Maddie asked the driver

"A good few minutes. We are waiting for this spot to open. My kid needs to go to the bathroom but wants a hot chocolate and muffin from this coffee shop," the driver responded.

"That vehicle has no placard or plates displaying their need for that spot," Maddie pointed out.

"I know, but the police won't come here for this, and they never really do anything about things like this. It seems like people see these parking spots as just a place they can park near the door and don't care that these are reserved for people with disabilities," the driver said, exasperated.

"That is absolutely disgusting! I'll wait here and say something to that person," Maddie exclaimed with fury.

Maddie stood by the SUV facing the coffee shop door with the snow blowing in nearly sideways. The slight pelting of the flakes on her face didn't make her flinch. They melted immediately as they contacted her heated face.

"Ugh! O-M-G!" she said in utter disbelief when a fully able-bodied man came out with a tray of various coffees. She approached him and said, "Excuse me, sir. Do you know you are parked in a spot designated for persons with disabilities?"

He was partially stunned but more irritated that this girl was questioning him. He cocked his phone down from his cheek to his chin and said, "Listen, little girl, I'm in a hurry, and I don't see anyone around here right now needing this spot. If you aren't the police, I'm going to go. Thank you for making me even more late." He moved his phone back up to his cheek and continued with his phone call while fumbling for his keys, saying, "Yeah, sorry about that, Tom. Yeah, some dumb little girl trying to be Portland Police or some shit. Yeah, I got your macchiato. Don't trip—it will still be hot when I get to the office."

"Um, actually, someone is waiting for this spot, you selfish jerk! Do you not see this van behind you over here?" she yelled at him.

He scoffed and gave a weak attempt at a look and continued to make no effort to show any care about the situation at hand.

Maddie was in disbelief as she watched him speed away without his seatbelt on and without stopping at the stop sign. She was still visibly shaking, and more so now than before. Before she began her slow trek to school, she walked by the van and gave the only response she could, a shaking of her head in pure disgust.

As she began to walk, the snow started to get heavier, and she was beginning to shake more from being cold and wet than from being infuriated by such a blatant asshole. She took a right near her middle school to retrace her route, but as she neared the school, she watched the hustle and bustle around her. She watched in amazement at all the business district activity while the last few vehicles were leaving her school in the distance from late drop-offs. She took note of gas stations full of cars, the busy dry cleaners, the cute animals going in and out of the pet store, and so many other shops filled with customers.

I love how they all seem like busy bees or ants. Everyone seems to be on a mission of survival. I love to see good, hard-working people. It's truly sad to see and hear the upper class and politicians talk about neighborhoods like this and how they are eyesores in the city. Without us, they wouldn't have their dry-cleaning services, house cleaners, mechanics, or anything like that. I'm still upset about them creating an ordinance to 'clean up' these areas. Sure, these apartment buildings and factories are old, but help us out, don't shove us out and build cookie-cutter homes to accommodate themselves, she thought as she tried to keep her mind busy from thinking of how cold she was.

She stayed in thought as she kept trudging along, ducking under overhangs to get some relief from the snow. With all these notices to vacate the apartments everywhere, we're not the only ones being forced to move. I wonder if Mom will commute or get a new job. Either way, it sucks to uproot all of these hard workers. And why? Because of an eyesore? My mom is an eyesore? If they really cared, they would find ways to help and not make us go to the outskirts of town or another city!

She was getting sick of the ignorance and hate in the area. She thought, how can anyone say that we aren't working-class citizens? We are the ones working in the restaurants, we are the ones cleaning bathrooms and offices, we are the ones operating the public transportation systems, we are the ones that deal with the garbage, we are the landscapers, we are the store clerks, we are the dry cleaners, we are mechanics, we are the workforce and do the work that they deem themselves above doing.

She went one more block and snapped out of her inner thoughts, ducking under the awning and into the local library. Maddie figured she'd warm up and hang up her coat to dry while she looked for some books to read over the next few weeks.

"Sweetie, there is a coat rack to your right," a voice chimed in from her left. This caught her off guard, and with a quick double blink of her eyelids, she shuffled sideways to the right and began to unzip her puffy jacket.

"Thank you," Maddie responded as she hung up her jacket and walked toward the front counter.

"It's freezing out there! What brings you in on such a blistering morning?" the typical librarian-looking lady asked as she beamed at Maddie over her glasses. The thin gold chain connected to the earpieces of her glasses swayed as she spoke.

I wish it was a blistering morning—like blistering that selfish asshole's ass, she said internally, still fuming about the man in the parking space.

"I'm looking to read up on something about karma or anything like that. I wouldn't even know where to begin," Maddie responded.

"Karma, huh? There is nothing about karma per se, but a few religions believe in something of the sort—but that's more for the afterlife. Is that something you would be interested in?" the librarian asked.

Maddie quickly responded: "Yeah, that sounds like a good start. I'm not a religious person, but I would like to read about that. What are these afterlife things?" she questioned with a sudden curiosity.

The librarian had a unique grin as she squinted over her glasses at this intrigued, eager learner.

"To sum it up: one believes that how you act and treat others, including nature, is how you'll be rewarded in your next life. For instance, if you are a good person and treat everyone and everything with love and respect, your next life will be blissful. The other believes that your actions will be judged in the afterlife, where you'll experience eternal bliss or eternal pain. But you must first go to a place called 'purgatory,' and you'll have to be cleansed of your transgressions. From there, you either go to paradise or eternal damnation," the librarian exclaimed in summary.

"Wait. So, with one, you get multiple chances and can come back, but the other is a one-shot deal?" an excited Maddie asked.

"Yes, but why don't you read a few books on each and read into it how you desire," an excited librarian responded.

Within minutes after their conversation, Maddie had a few books at the counter and was ready to check out.

"When you finish up with those, come on back. I can try to get some new books in by then, if you'd like," the librarian gleefully offered.

"That would be great. And thank you," Maddie said as she finished putting the books in her backpack and got her puffy jacket on.

"Well, back out into the blistering morning," Maddie said with a smile.

With that, she was bundled up and heading back out into the elements. Luckily for Maddie, she was close to home. The snowfall became heavier as she trudged through the drifts piling up on the sidewalks.

She began to converse in her mind as her steps became more labored. *At least there aren't as many vehicles on the road right now. I'm excited to snuggle up at home while I read through these books. I wish I could find out what happens to these crazy drivers. At least after we move, we will never have to deal with these people again. I just hope Mom moves us into an area where folks are genuine and nicer, but I'm sure we'll still have selfish and self-righteous jerks anywhere we go. I guess we can only wait and see.*

Shortly after Maddie finished her thoughts, she opened the apartment complex door.

"Oh yes! Finally, time to get warm and relax," she said as she pressed the button to the elevator. "Oh, it's still on the ninth floor? This janky-ass elevator will take forever!" she continued.

Just as she said that and started to the stairs, she got a confused and dirty look from an elderly lady standing and reading her mail by the mailboxes.

"What the hell is that lady looking at?" she muttered. "Kids cuss all the time nowadays. Who the hell cares? We hear it from them, anyway. Oh well, I'm looking forward to some hot cocoa and my heated blanket while I read this shit!" she said, winded from talking aloud as she skipped every other step in her hurry.

"Maddie. Maddie. Wake up," a motherly voice said.

"Ugh! What time is it?" Maddie replied with a groggy voice and blurred vision

"It's five-thirty. You need to get up, or you won't sleep at all tonight. I don't even need to ask how long you've been here. The school called me at work. You missed the whole day. Lucky for you, one of the neighbors saw you come into the building," her mom said.

Maddie didn't even respond. She sat there with eyes wide open and making long slow blinks to try and comprehend the lecture she knew was coming. Sure enough, Maddie's mom began her speech about the importance of not missing school anymore. She only caught small tidbits of it.

"...and by missing even one day, you'll get behind, and it's hard to catch up," Maddie's mom continued as she paced in the apartment living room.

Maddie sat there and nodded as her mom occasionally looked over to see if she was listening. Maddie continued to blink at her slender and tall mom. She began to let her mind drift while her mom talked about how her brother and sister don't skip school and how important it is to keep good grades, be social, and play sports for their futures. *I wonder if Mom is thinner than most women her age because of metabolism, stress, lengthy working hours, or dieting? Could be a mix of it all. Maybe one day we will find out.*

"Are you even listening to me?" her mom asked, snapping Maddie's attention back to her.

"Yes, Mother. I have heard this speech a hundred thousand times before. Now it's a hundred thousand and one. 'Be more like Megan and Mark. Be popular like them. Play sports. Get better grades.' I know—I heard it all. I'm glad I haven't been like them because we all have to make new friends soon anyway. So why start now?" Maddie responded with a bit of sarcasm.

Her mom snapped back with frustration, "I know we have to leave here soon, but you could have gained those life skills. Those skills will transfer into wherever life takes us next and beyond that. Please work on it. I only want you to be happy, healthy, and successful. Now, go do your homework and try not to get behind again. I love you."

As Maddie sat at the dining room table with her homework out, she heard the ever-familiar sound of the answering machine starting to play messages. It wasn't until the third message that Maddie heard something she wasn't keen on.

Beep. "Uh, hi. This is John at Lazy Lemons Law Firm. This message is for Melanie. We were very impressed with your resume and your interview. We would like you to start as our new secretary starting on Monday. We will pay you triple what you are making now. Have a great day, and we look forward to seeing you Monday morning at eight."

Maddie's mom, Mel, stopped playing the messages and did a little dance, running in place while spinning in circles. Maddie's little sister Megan came over to hug her. Megan and Mel shed tears of joy.

"Maddie, honey. Did you hear that?" Mel asked.

"I sure did, Mom," Maddie responded blandly.

"You don't seem too enthused by this," Mel said with a puzzled look.

"I'm happy for you, Mom, but I don't want you to be like those rich people who look down on us. The ones that are kicking us out of *our* homes. Or the ones that drive fancy cars, speed through our neighborhood, and blow through the stop signs by our schools. Please don't become one of those people. Promise me, Mom," Maddie said with the most concern Mel had ever heard from her oldest daughter.

Mel responded to Maddie's concern, "Oh, honey. I hear your concern and am glad you expressed it to me. I promise to try and never become tha—"

"No. Don't promise that you'll try. Promise that you won't become one of them," Maddie interrupted emphatically.

"Okay, honey. I promise that I *won't* become one of them," Mel promised with assurance. She continued, "This is exciting because

I have worked so hard to make everything happen for you kids, and we will now have some breathing room. The hard work doesn't stop, though. This is just the universe acknowledging and rewarding me for all my efforts and all the love I have for you guys. Things are looking up for us!"

"Maddie, honey. We have been out here in the southern suburbs of Portland for about five years now, and you still have yet to really be social or play sports. I know your grades have been great since moving here, but not being social won't get you too far. Before you graduate, you should probably come out of your shell and get out more," Mel started the familiar lecture to her oldest daughter.

"Maybe I'll socialize more when you stop being what you promised me you wouldn't be," Maddie said to her mom with a bit of an attitude.

"What do you mean? I promised not to become one of *them*," Mel snapped back.

"You're driving a luxury foreign fancy car. You have fancy and shiny jewelry and an expensive watch. You've totally become one of them," Maddie said with disappointment.

"Honey, just because I have treated myself for working hard and saving doesn't mean that I'm one of them. I don't act like the people that you've described. I'm pretty modest and treat people how I would want you all to be treated," Mel explained. She continued, "Haven't you heard the old saying, 'Don't judge a book by its cover'? It means—"

"I know what it means, Mom. You should treat yourself, but I'm just concerned that these things might turn you into that evil. You know the old saying, 'money is the root of all evil'?" Maddie lectured.

"Yes, honey. I know that one too. I appreciate your concern, and I love you for expressing it. No need to lecture me, though. I love you." Mel finalized the conversation with a look at her watch.

Mel's last sentence and seeing the watch made Maddie get up and put on her light jacket to begin her trek to the local hole-in-the-wall used bookstore a little over two miles away. Maddie was just glad to be out in the spring sun and absorbed the rays as she thought about karma and the dozens of books she'd read about it over the past few years.

She is right, though, she thought as she continued walking to Used Books Plus.

She has worked hard and taken great care of Megan, Mark, and me. She does deserve nice things to reward herself for her hard work and sacrifices. I just hope it doesn't go too far and she breaks her promise. Is there a line between good and bad karma? How does one define good and bad karma? And who determines good and bad karma, anyway? Wouldn't someone think that most things they do are "good" from their own perspective?

CHAPTER TWO

"HEY, MA! YOU'RE home early!" AJ said as her mom startled her with the closing of the side door.

"Me? You're home early too. What are you doing at home?" AJ's mom said back in surprise but with her witty smirk.

"Finals week," AJ said as she continued to make her turkey sandwich with mayo, honey mustard, a cold tomato, and a slice of Colby Jack cheese.

"Ah. I see," her ma said. "How are finals? Any plans after graduation?"

AJ finished the delicious initial bite of her sandwich and said, "I've been working hard and saving up a bit. I want to travel to a place where I can explore some supernatural locations. Now, before you say anything, I know I'm weird for liking that stuff. It really intrigues me. There have never been real answers on what happens when we die. We just have to believe in something. I know our family's values on this, but I just want to explore for myself."

Her mom gave her a half-cocked grin and crossed her arms while waiting for more.

"I'm waiting for Amy to call me back to see if she can pick up some of my shifts. Then when I get back, Josh said I can pick up some of his shifts so he can take some extra time this summer. I'll buy all of my books in advance. Don't worry about that, Ma. I'm getting everything covered," AJ explained.

With that bit of comfort, her ma uncrossed her arms and walked around the counter to AJ to give her a side hug and say, "I know you are responsible, baby. It's just that you're my baby, and it's tough to see you graduating and going off to college."

"I know, Ma, but I got everything covered, and I'll tell you all the travel info and keep you in the loop every day," she said to give her mom more comfort.

With that, her ma left the kitchen, and AJ finished her lunch and headed into her room to work on more planning.

AJ was born and raised in Grand Rapids, Michigan. She was the youngest of her siblings and had always been a jet-setter but modest and humble. Being the youngest, she'd grown up tough. Watching both of her parents working hard to make enough for bills, college funds, and some vacations, she noticed the value of hard work. She even noticed her siblings working at local restaurants as teenagers to help her parents cover their car notes and insurance, plus a little extra cash. AJ noticed these things and adopted the same ethics.

AJ had always been easygoing and was the natural comedian of whatever group she was with. It was hard to tell if she was stressed, anxious, or annoyed. Since AJ could remember, she had always been enticed by the aspects of the universe that are beyond the grasp of a human hand. She watched many television shows, movies, and documentaries about the otherworldly. She never wanted to use a Ouija Board, or anything of that nature, to explore the potential other side because she was always cautious about those things out of fear of being possessed or even worse. So, she just stuck with watching everything she could about the unknown and unexplained. AJ would frighten herself by staying up late watching shows like *Unsolved Mysteries*. Her mother would ask her why she would watch a show about aliens, abductions, missing persons, hauntings, and ever murders, before going to bed.

With the advancement of the internet, she had these shows,

documentaries, movies, and books at her fingertips. Around her friends, she never really let on that this fascinated her. She'd instead talk about sports or whatever the daily topics were. As she had grown older and prepared to enter a local junior college, she wanted to learn more and explore the lands to see if others had the same interests.

She thought, *Others have to be just as interested in the unknown. There has to be a big enough audience for such great shows, docuseries, documentaries, movies, books, and news coverage. One day soon, I'll go visit some haunted hotels and find some other cool places where unexplained events occur.*

AJ was the last of her siblings to graduate from high school, and her family celebrated with many tears of joy mixed with a touch of sadness. Their baby was now all grown up and anxious to explore the world and the great unknown. It seemed like no sooner after her big graduation party than she was sitting in a college summer school class trying to get a jump on her soon-to-be classmates. A fierce competitor, AJ wanted to gain an edge in the freshman class. She took two prerequisite classes to gain such an edge. While that occupied some of her time, she researched haunted locations around the nation and the cheapest methods of transportation and lodging while she was there.

"Hey, sweetie?" her ma said as she poked her head through AJ's door.

"Yeah, Ma!" AJ responded with her back to her doorway.

"I came by to see what you would want for dinner but now am curious as to what you are doing?" her ma asked.

"Oh, this? I'm hanging up a map on my wall. I picked it up at the gas station on the way home. One of those Rand McNally maps you and Pa are always talking about," AJ responded with her back still to her door and mother.

Even more curious, her mom stepped in and asked, "You know that you can use the tacks on the corners to hold it up? Like a normal way of doing something like this. I know you know how to do that.

I see your music posters hanging just fine."

AJ responded with some tacks in her mouth, "I know, Ma, but there is a method to this madness. I'm hanging the map up with color coordination. With all of the research that I have done, I have it all color-coded. Almost like a traffic light coordination."

AJ turned to show her ma the tacks she had already inserted while working on getting a few more spread out. "See, the tacks are coded by my interest in the location and affordability. The various shades of green mean the likelihood of being able to afford the trip, the time I'll need to spend, and my interest in that specific area. The lighter the color means the more chance of going. Obviously, the red is a no-go, but that is based mostly on cost, the time I would need to spend there, and maybe the reviews. I know it sounds crazy, but that's the best visual I could create. The spreadsheet is good, but this is better for my brain."

"That's not crazy at all, sweetie. I love it, and if it helps you make a well-educated decision and makes you happy, then I'm all for it. Now, maybe you can color-code a decision on what you want for dinner," her ma said with a smile.

"I don't need to color-code that decision. How about your famous fried chicken and mashed taters?" AJ said, and they both chuckled. With that, her ma left AJ to her task while she tried to relax a bit before the rest of the family got home.

AJ would have three weeks between summer classes and the start of her first semester of college. Although most of her classes would be the basic requirements for her upper-division courses, she didn't want to discount those courses. She also wanted to explore and decompress a bit between courses. Between the money she had received for her graduation and working, she decided that she would just go on an adventure for about a week, depending on the cost.

She jotted down some of the lighter green locations to ensure they would still be affordable. She searched and searched and was disappointed with what she found. The prices were nearly doubled from when she had started her map in the early spring. She yelled in a low voice at the computer, "Are you freaking kidding me? This is such bullshit! How can the airlines do this to people? I understand supply and demand, but this is straight-up robbery! The summer months and holidays are when most of the working folks can take time off. This is just a slap in the face for the everyday worker!"

She walked away from the computer for nearly an hour to grab another sandwich and talk to one of her friends about the whole thing. Her friend asked her if it would be worth it to escape for a bit and to explore, especially without her family. AJ tried to say, "Yeah, it would be," as she chomped on her cold turkey and cheese sandwich. AJ washed it down with a cool carbonated swig of her favorite pop and continued with, "It would be worth it. I haven't been out of the area since we all went on a family vacation three years ago to Myrtle Beach. Plus, I haven't been out West. We've only been throughout the Midwest and the East Coast, anywhere that was drivable because gas is cheaper than airline tickets for a family of five."

She went back into her room so she could refresh her search on the travel company's website. While she did that, she loaded up her bank's website to double-check that everything would be fine and to ensure some extra money for sightseeing and any possible emergencies. She was good for that price and even had some extra for emergencies. The trip was two-and-a-half weeks away, and she'd be gone for one week. That would leave her two weeks between her trip and the start of her first semester.

She wrote all her plans in her handy notebook, on a sticky for the fridge, and in an email that she'd have ready for her parents, just in case. With all of that out of the way, she refreshed the page again and began looking at the prices, the time of travel, and what cities she'd be laying over in.

Leaving from Grand Rapids meant that she'd have to have a layover somewhere that was a hub for a major airline like New York, Chicago, Atlanta, Detroit, Denver, Houston, Dallas, DC, or

Minneapolis. Five of those she'd be able to just drive to if it brought down the cost significantly. To her, the point was to explore and set out on a big fun adventure where she didn't have to work—and those drives would be work.

She kept looking, and some prices and times had aligned for at least the trip out West. If this flight worked out just right, she'd be able to have a good layover in Minneapolis during the day and would be able to see a little bit of the city. She clicked it and opened up options for the return flight. She looked at her options and selected the night flight to Atlanta, which would allow her a few hours in Atlanta to get a quick breakfast outside the airport and experience the area a bit.

She clicked to select the Atlanta red-eye as her return. She saw the price again before she entered her information as the passenger. When she entered her information and clicked to select seats, a page popped up asking her if she wanted to pay more for add-ons. This really made AJ mad. As she looked at the price of these add-ons, she practically had a panic attack.

Can't I just get in my seat and get to my destination? Where the hell is all this money going, anyway? I always see the news reports about how the backbones of these companies are making very little, and yet the CEOs are getting tens of millions of dollars for end-of-year bonuses. Shit, when they get fired, they still get a severance package of tens of millions of dollars. This is why. They rob their passengers and their employees! So sickening and wrong!

After she reread everything and made sure that she didn't have to pay for the add-ons, she continued to pick her seats. She figured she'd sit somewhere in the middle of the plane and bring a book and music to relax. She finalized all the typing, double-checked everything, took a deep breath, and moved the cursor over the *complete purchase* button. She let out her breath and said, "What the hell! Let's freaking go!" and clicked the button.

Maddie had been in Used Books Plus for nearly two hours. She thought, *This spring day is beautiful, but the daylight barely makes it through the small windows in here. It's like one of those old Las Vegas casinos where they intentionally keep the daylight out, so you have very little idea of how long you've been in there.*

Maddie continued in thought, *This store is so fascinating. I love the wide variety of genres here; historical books, books on the cosmos, books about creepy lawn gnomes coming to life, comics, books about religion, and even stuff about the supernatural.*

One store worker was intrigued by Maddie as she rummaged through the books. After being in the store for nearly two hours, it was obvious that Maddie didn't have just one subject of interest. She went through piles of books and created her own stack of titles she wanted to look closer at. Maddie didn't look like an athlete, but the store clerk saw some crazy strength in her as she moved piles of books to get to the others she just skimmed over. As it neared closing time, the clerk went over to notify Maddie that the store would be closing in fifteen minutes but that she didn't have to leave until the clerk needed to head out thirty minutes after closing. Maddie nodded and got back into reading the back covers of books and the foreword sections.

Twenty minutes after closing, the clerk slowly walked up to Maddie and admired her passion for reading. She continued to slowly approach as she softly spoke to her. "We have to get going today, but if you want, we can set aside your books, and you can buy whatever ones you want today. You can come back any time, and those books won't move. It's not like many folks come through here anyway."

Maddie stood up and grabbed the top three books on her stack, putting them with the one she had started to read. She walked to the counter with her four books and the clerk. The clerk rang up her books and said, "That will be eight dollars and seventy-six cents."

Maddie looked stunned and excitedly gasped, "Only eight dollars and seventy-six cents? Whoa! That's awesome cheap! These four books would be well over fifty dollars brand new, easy."

The clerk was happy to see the excitement from Maddie. She reached across the counter to give Maddie her change. She set it in her hand and then kept her hand out to shake her hand. In the same motion she said, "I'm Machelle. It's a pleasure to finally meet someone with the same enthusiasm about books as me."

Maddie held the money and slightly raised her hand in a wave. "Maddie. It's nice to meet you too."

Maddie didn't know why Machelle was so cheerful and wanted to converse beyond typical courtesies, but she went with it. As Machelle came around the counter to walk out and lock up the front door upon their exit, she began to chat with Maddie. "Not too many people come into the store, and it's rare for any to stay as long as you did. Typically people come in and seem to be in a hurry to find a specific book or genre of books. I noticed you have a variety of books in your stack to come back to. I really like the books you bought today. One of them is a favorite of mine."

Maddie looked down at the four books in confusion because she had forgotten which books she bought because this overly cheerful clerk kept rambling on and on. As they stood under the door light, she looked down at the books while Machelle locked up and tilted her head to also take a look. "This one! This one is great and my favorite."

Maddie kind of shrugged it off and turned to start walking when Machelle asked, "Hey, Maddie, want a ride? It's almost dark, and it's supposed to be a cold one tonight. And a storm is supposed to be rolling in soon."

Maddie squinted and looked at the road she had walked earlier in the bright sunlight, noticing the lack of cars on the now darkened street. She checked her light coat and thought, *A nice heated ride would be good but not this overly cheerful, one-sided conversation.* With her back to Machelle, she lightly shouted back in an almost instant regret, "Yeah, thanks. I only live a few miles from here."

This added to Machelle's excitement level. "Yay!" she cheered with high-pitched glee. "Hop in." She got in and started the engine to get it warmed up. She unlocked the door and plugged her cell phone in, and they sat there for a minute. Machelle kept thinking of tons of questions while Maddie wondered, *Why the hell aren't we driving? We could almost be there by now.*

As soon as the car was warm, they began the quick drive to Maddie's house. Maddie guided Machelle down the road and thought, *Who the hell just offers a ride to someone they just met, especially at night on a dark road? I sure hope she doesn't ask me too many more questions.*

No sooner than she'd thought that, Machelle chirped a line of questions, "Why those four books? You had a whole stack? I mean, those books are great but why just those? Are you interested in those subjects, or are you just trying to read something outside of required school reading? Either way, you'll find them fascinating. Let me know what you think when you come back."

They pulled into the driveway of Maddie's house. Mel came to the window to see who had pulled into her driveway. She was taken aback and excited to see Maddie get out of the car. She didn't want to seem like she was prying, so she quickly stepped away and walked back into the kitchen area to get Maddie some dinner and to clean up.

Maddie went to close the door, and Machelle said, "I'll keep your book stack safe for when you come back. You're welcome back anytime, and I'll have more of those types of books ready for ya."

Maddie nodded and said, "Thank you, and thank you for the ride," as she got out of the car and closed the door.

Machelle drove off, and Maddie walked in from the chilly dark evening, setting her books down on the kitchen island. Her mom smiled and said, "So . . . who is your friend?"

Maddie said, "She's not my friend. She is the clerk from the used bookstore down the road."

"Well, you were gone for some time. Were you at the store the whole time?"

"Yeah. This store has a lot of old, intriguing books."

Mel walked over to the books and read them, saying, "These are old books. The binding is old, and the pages look a bit frail. Books on Catholic beliefs about purgatory. Black magic. Witchcraft. And, what's this one—Karma?"

Dan was walking with his dog one evening, as usual. He loved taking his dog on walks this time of the evening for the view of the skies. Plus, it gave his dog, an eighty-pound English Golden Retriever named Juliet, a little exercise after her dinner and before they went to bed. He'd been taking her on a nightly walk for four years, ever since she was a puppy. Throughout those years he had seen some great sunsets, and he loved how the city and suburbs would get dark, but the sky would still stay so lit and slowly change colors. Soon after the sunset, the sky would change from orange to a reddish tint and then into pink and purple before transitioning into the beautiful black skies dotted with the light from the brightest stars that could pierce the city lights throughout San Diego County.

On this particular evening, the sun had set beautifully on the Pacific Ocean. Dan and Juliet were walking westward and could see the massive sun as it set into the blue depths of the sea. The sky started its change, as there were no clouds in view, except for toward the east, where the mountains had clouds harassing the peaks. Dan particularly liked this time of year because it was just after daylight saving time and not yet time for the usual marine layer that would roll in during the evening hours of May and June. This time of year was great for Dan's mind because the plants blooming, the birds chirping, and the extended daylight hours allowed him to unwind on these walks with Juliet and just observe the life evolving around him.

Dan worked a typical nine-to-five job that allowed for plenty of options for travel. He worked as an adviser on a committee in the city. His job was unique, as he worked with many companies and the local military bases to ensure that their wants and needs were expressed during city meetings. He worked hard to do his due diligence to ensure everyone was happy and the city remained a great place for locals to stay, outsiders to want to visit, and companies to continue to operate here. Dan was a midwesterner but had found this job by accident and accepted it as he was growing tired of the hot, humid summers and freezing winters in St. Louis. He frequently traveled back home to see family, get some great home-cooked meals, and see his beloved sports teams.

As a big sports fan, he began following local teams throughout the San Diego region and bought season tickets to all of them. That helped him socialize and also ensured he saw how the city reacted to the sports teams. He tried not to work while at the sporting events, but being a very thorough individual, he couldn't help but notice certain things. He also followed the team's fan pages to see any complaints about the stadiums, arenas, fields, or the surrounding areas. He also noted whether changes were made in those regards and in a timely manner. This was particularly fun for him as he enjoyed a drink or two while cheering on his new teams and socializing with other fans. It was relaxing to him to enjoy the company of others that thoroughly enjoyed a sport as much as he did.

It was just about the time when the sky was still light enough to not yet see all the stars out, but a few of the brightest in the sky had started to shine through. Dan and his pup were still walking toward the horizon. They were just a few blocks away from their usual turnaround point from which they would return home, fix some quick dinner, and watch some shows to relax before calling it a night.

Dan had witnessed some crazy and impatient drivers on this particularly busy road. He had always wondered why people had to drive like such crazies. Surely they all couldn't be in a medical emergency. So, why would these people need to be so impatient and in such a hurry? It boggled his mind. In an attempt to not be annoyed, stressed, frustrated, or worried, he made up a little game and tried to see the face of the driver. To better play this game, he would try to see their facial expressions, what they looked like, if they were on the phone (either on a call or texting), or if they had someone else in the vehicle. He would make up funny stories about why they had such angry eyebrows or why their veins were popping out of their temples or necks.

He would think, *Oh, that guy thinks he is getting lucky tonight. That lady is pissed at her husband. That mom is about to whip her kid's ass.* Although they would go speeding by, he would take notice of the vehicles and any identifying markers. The one thing that really pissed him off was seeing school magnets on vehicles and vehicles with car seats in them as they sped well over the posted speed limits.

He would think to himself, *What kind of irresponsible person would knowingly put their own flesh and blood at risk of injury or death because they failed to plan properly? How could you risk your kid's life to try and get somewhere thirty seconds or so faster than you would if you drove safely? You're already late, so why not get there safely and late as opposed to not arriving at all?*

Although he tried to only think of the positive aspects of his nightly walk, like the great sunsets, he would still see these kinds of irresponsible parents zoom by, and it would get his blood boiling.

Dan and Juliet were less than a block away from the turnaround point. This area had a nice white wall with bronze coloring on the big letters boasting the neighborhood name. A few feet in front of the wall were small lights that would turn on when the natural lighting dimmed to a certain level.

Besides being a good and visible spot for Dan to turn around, he liked looking into the community to see the fancy sports cars in the driveways of the big homes. He would wonder what the people in that neighborhood did to earn so much money to live in those big mansions and drive such excellent sports cars. He loved seeing the whole variety of sports cars from the 1950s to recent model years.

As he and Juliet stood on the inside of the corner facing

southwest, admiring the vast array of sports cars, they heard tires squealing from about a mile away. With the sound of the exhaust and the headlights rapidly approaching, he thought he'd be witnessing a street race or a high-speed chase.

He stood in place and held Juliet's leash tight as she sat there with him, eyeballing a bird moving in the tree above them. The headlights grew brighter and faster as the engine revved noticeably louder. As the car gained speed, now beyond even a reckless level, it didn't slow at the start of the slow uphill left turn on the two-lane road. The vehicle appeared to be heading straight for the wall with no signs of stopping.

Dan grabbed Juliet and took off running to get away from any shrapnel radius. He hoped this was just an overreaction on his part, but he was not taking any chances. He kept running south, downhill, while trying to look over his shoulder at the driver's state, if there were passengers, and if the vehicle had any signs of slowing down. Was something wrong with the accelerator? As he ran, he fumbled to get his camera on his phone to get open and to video to record this soon-to-be catastrophe. He caught the last eight seconds.

The white sedan kept speeding without any signs of stopping. He saw three White males in what appeared to be their late twenties. They were dressed businesslike but didn't have any distinguishing details about them. As Dan ran with his camera recording and trying to get clear of any possible damage to him and his dog, he noticed that the three men had their eyes closed as if they were sleeping, but their heads remained upright. He didn't think anything of it at the time as he tried to put more ground between him and the debris field. He turned to look over his shoulder one last time before impact, again hoping he would see the car swerve and speed off. He let out a ghastly yell as he watched the car and its occupants completely disappear.

CHAPTER THREE

B etween the spring and the summer months, Maddie spent her
weekends reading books she got from Used Books Plus. Each
time she finished her stack of books, she enjoyed the walk back to
the bookstore.

"You know, I really like all the visits," Machelle said as Maddie
walked in. She continued when Maddie gave her a confused glance,
"The visits you make when you come back for more books. I had
a shipment of a few that came in specifically for your 'to buy' pile."

As a token of her appreciation, Maddie usually conversed with
Machelle. This was a unique building of a friendship, but it was, in
fact, a friendship.

One early Sunday afternoon, Machelle asked Maddie, "May I ask
a personal question?"

"Yeah, sure. What's up?" Maddie replied in confusion as she
skimmed through a book.

Before Machelle could ask, Maddie thought, *What the hell could
she ask? She already knows my name, my book interests, where I live,
and what I like to eat.*

After mulling it over and seeing that Maddie didn't even look
up to give her full attention to the question, she asked, "So why the
books on these specific topics? This is some deep stuff, and not too
many people are as curious as you are about the subjects."

Maddie stopped reading through the book on the Catholic
church's ancient beliefs about purgatory, blinked a few times in

thought, and then slowly swiveled around in the chair. She thought about the selfish and cruel people in the world before responding.

She spoke softly but with a fiery passion. "Because the world is full of awful people that only think for themselves. I watched hundreds of people get uprooted, and their lives turned upside down because people were inconvenienced by looking at them and their living situations. People that throw money at problems. People that complain about homelessness but don't offer any support. People that commit the worst crimes and get away with it. People that change and become horrible people because of money and fame."

She continued as her voice raised with passion, but she was careful not to include her personal encounters. "I want to know if those people get what they deserve. Do they get to waste away in purgatory thinking about their transgressions while they suffer?"

Machelle's eyes grew wide as she focused on this newly revealed side of Maddie. She didn't have to ask for any personal reasons, as she could see and hear the passion. Machelle nodded in agreement and thought of her own personal encounters with the world's evilness while she watched Maddie slowly swivel back to her book. She thought about some examples to share with Maddie and what she hoped would happen to them. She wanted Maddie to know that she had been through some terrible things, too, and would like her to have that odd comfort in knowing she wasn't alone.

Machelle proceeded, "I didn't always work here. I worked at a convenience store and was robbed at gunpoint. The guy who robbed me, well, the convenience store, was caught a few miles down the road passed out with a needle hanging out of his arm. He was a multi-offense criminal and junkie who robbed the store for the forty-six dollars in the register to then just go shoot up some methamphetamine. He risked lives to get a quick fix. He was only sentenced to six months in jail and was then released on good behavior."

Maddie was intrigued and wanted to hear more stories. She opened up, and they volleyed stories for about an hour. She shared stories of the upper-class business types speeding through her old neighborhood, splashing cold, snowy, and muddy pothole water on young elementary school kids as they ran stop signs in the school zones. Machelle wondered how long it had taken for those poor kids to get warm and dry after such incidents. It must have been hours. That sort of stuff had their blood boiling as they talked. As they shared stories, they hoped for long-lasting justice—the kind that would educate people and make the world a better place.

They fantasized about the person who had splashed those kids suffering in purgatory the same way he had made others suffer. So he would get splashed and be wet and freezing cold for the same amount of time it had taken for one kid to dry off and warm up, and then have it done over and over again for all the kids he had done this to. Once he finally finished that punishment, he'd transfer into the next major wrongdoing and have to feel the pain of that person or persons.

They both agreed that there would have to be some serious transgressions for someone to end up in purgatory. They also agreed that people make honest mistakes, lose focus, or get complacent, and one wrongdoing here and there wouldn't deserve a trip to such a hell.

This made them both think of karma and whether good and bad karma does, in fact, catch up to people. In their curiosity, they began researching some cases where karma may have affected some people. They saw politicians being ousted for affairs, corruption, blackmail, and bribery, but that didn't really give them enough statistical information, as they both knew that many politicians were corrupt and easily bought out. They looked through news articles and saw gang members on trial for murders and human and drug trafficking. They saw individuals of positional authority physically and sexually abusing youths that had been convicted, were still on trial, or had already been released from custody. They found articles on drunk drivers on their fourth DUI, killing entire families. They saw newspaper clippings of real estate frauds. They even saw scumbags on news clips crying in court only after they'd been convicted and sentenced for tragic crimes.

It was really depressing to see how horrible the world had become and how people only seemed to be remorseful when they were caught. Until then, they continued to carry on their selfish behavior. This was truly sending Machelle and Maddie's moods into a downward spiral. Before closing up, they began searching for uplifting news stories about dogs being adopted from shelters, teenagers finding and returning sums of money they had found, or students volunteering to pick up trash along the river's edge on their day off from school. This sort of news helped them get into a better mindset for the rest of the day.

They had both had enough of the research and trying to figure out what happens to people who do bad things when they die—one of life's longest and biggest mysteries.

Machelle broke the tired silence, asking, "So what about your brother?"

"What about him?" Maddie shot back in tired confusion.

"I mean, he's cute. Like, does he have a girlfriend?" Machelle asked with a peppy smile.

Maddie squinted at her friend to get a read on her and to configure an answer. After a few seconds she responded, "I guess he's single."

"You guess?" Machelle asked in an even more confused tone than Maddie's.

"Yeah, I guess. I don't ask him about his love life. Even if he talks about it at dinner or when we all hang out, I tune it all out," Maddie explained.

"Well, does he bring any girls around? Or talk about girls?" Machelle asked more inquisitively.

Annoyed by the line of questioning and seemingly endless pursuit of nonsense, Maddie snapped back: "Look, I don't hear any names. I don't see any girl around, either. Plus, he is only a junior in high school. Aren't you, like, a freshman in college?"

As Maddie turned her direction back into her open book, she whispered, "I wouldn't even notice anyway."

Machelle knew the conversation, at least that part, was over. She then got back into the books with a cheeky grin and let it be.

◇————————————◇

As the spring days slowly edged to summer, Maddie and Machelle delved deeper into various books as their research on karma continued. Maddie was in her senior year of high school and only had four classes during her last semester. This allowed her to spend from lunchtime until after Used Books Plus closed with Machelle. During the hours that Maddie was in class, Machelle would work on finding more books around the world on those subjects and had books dropped off every day at the store. Machelle would spend hours on the computer searching local listings in regions of the world that she had never even dreamed of visiting. Sometimes she would use an online translator to copy and paste certain words into the search box. If it looked like a possible match, she would use the translation system to dive in deeper.

Together they could skim through a few hundred books each month. Maddie's mom was really happy about this newfound friendship. Even though she only had a small idea of the depth of the relationship, she was happy that Maddie wasn't being reclusive and weird. She just knew that reading books and having a social life was a positive way for Maddie to consume her time while Mel was working. This also helped settle Mel's anxieties about Maddie growing up and not having any transition after high school.

One early afternoon as Maddie was nearing finals week, she went home instead of walking the short distance from the high school to Used Books Plus. To her surprise, she noticed Machelle sitting on her porch, waiting impatiently for her to arrive from school. Maddie furrowed her eyebrows and thought, *"Witchcraft! How in the actual hell did she know that I would be here instead of the bookstore?"*

Machelle noticed the confusion, the slight anger, and even the line of questions that would soon occur if she didn't just get straight to it.

"You have to come with me to the store!" Machelle urged.

"What are you doing here? Are you here for my brother?" Maddie asked half-jokingly.

"No. I'm here for you. You have to come with me to the store," Machelle said with a renewed sense of urgency.

"I have finals next week and need to study. I'm sorry, but I can't," Maddie replied in an annoyed tone.

"No, Maddie, you have to come with me," she pleaded.

"Machelle, I need to take two weeks off and focus on school so I can graduate and be done. I can jump back into our research after," Maddie explained as she tried to walk around her and into the house.

Machelle quickly sidestepped to her right on the porch and stood directly toe to toe with Maddie. Maddie could see and feel the desperation in Machelle's expressions and mannerisms. As they locked eyes and the sky grew darker, Machelle said, "Please come with me to the store. It's very vital."

Maddie nodded and agreed but wanted to go in and drop her school stuff off, get her books from her room, and get something to drink. Afterward, they walked to the car with their drinks and Maddie's books. The late spring sky was growing darker with what appeared to be thunderstorms rolling into the area. As they drove through the streets and the clouds grew darker, they didn't speak. Machelle wasn't very chatty, which was odd. This confused Maddie as she kept trying to glance at Machelle and get a read on her.

Within minutes they were pulling up to the store. As they got under the awning and Machelle unlocked the door, the sky opened up, and it started to rain. Maddie noticed that Machelle didn't disarm the alarm. *She must have left in a hurry earlier,* Maddie thought, puzzled by this new, weird behavior. As they walked in, she noticed that Machelle locked the door behind them and flipped the *open* sign to *closed.* She was also puzzled as to why she only turned the lights on dim instead of on normal. She followed Machelle around with a puzzled look as she maneuvered in a manner unlike her normal self. As they walked through the dimly lit bookstore, Maddie was startled to see someone in dark clothes sitting by a desk upon which a very old book sat. Two empty chairs were pulled up to the desk.

Kyle stood about five foot seven and always had his hair slicked back from the front left side of his forehead to behind his right ear. His friends teased him about having to get a second job to support his hair product addiction. This pissed him off a little bit, but he took pride in his hair and his look. Kyle could typically be found in a few spots: the gym (of course), the club, the bar, or driving his Bro Dozer look-alike from Orlando to one of the beaches nearby.

Kyle's Bro Dozer was a big, lifted full-cab truck with big mud tires so ridiculous that they stuck out and severely crushed his gas mileage. He didn't care about gas mileage. But he did care about his look, and no one better ever dare to flip his flat-bill trucker-style local beer company hat and mess up his hair. He'd even gotten into a fistfight once with one of his former friends in a bar for doing that one time. Kyle was pissed because he thought it had ruined his chance with the chick he was talking up at the bar.

Kyle could be found heading out of Orlando as soon as he was done taking "Flex Friday" selfies at the gym. He typically tried to get to work earlier on his arm workout days so he could beat the evening gym rush. He hated it when the evening gym rush took up his time with arm workouts in front of the mirrors. On leg day, he didn't mind the gym rush because if he couldn't get in on a machine, he'd go talk to the hottie on one of the leg workout machines nearby. He wore compression pants to make his legs appear bigger, among other things, but they also conveniently covered up his steroid injection marks.

His gym shirts weren't shirts at all—or at least they used to be, but he had cut most of them so that they barely covered his upper body. He liked to think he was showing off his muscles, but, in all reality, he was unknowingly airing out his body odor.

Kyle knew just about every party beach on every coast in Florida. He lived for the weekend and drunk chicks. His friends mostly thought he was an all-right guy that just liked to party and was misunderstood. They told people he could be a cool guy and was just a "bro's bro." Even though they stood up for him, he had gone through many friends throughout his life. He may not show it on the outside, but it did bother him. He always blamed them, and his other bros always lifted him up and told him that he was better off without them, that they just weren't cool enough to hang out with his crew. Then they'd just crash another beach party and drink enough to temporarily forget about it.

Throughout Kyle's whole life, he had suffered from sleep paralysis. He had always told his mom and dad that he had periods of being awake yet couldn't move and felt like a demonic spirit was haunting him. They brought in a priest to bless every house they had ever lived in, but it still happened. Kyle would just get up and start doing a workout as if to say, "Screw you, demon! I'm stronger than you! If you want to fight, reveal your bitch-ass self!" But nothing ever appeared.

As an adult, Kyle read about being possessed by a demonic spirit but never had those signs or symptoms. He definitely didn't have it bad enough to bring in a Catholic priest to do an exorcism. He did watch all of the cool movies on exorcisms but was freaked out to know that some of those movies were based on true stories. He knew he didn't meet the criteria for such actions, but he kept researching and finally went to a doctor to discuss it. It was the doctor who had figured out that he suffered from sleep paralysis.

He did an internet search on sleep paralysis and felt relieved to know that he was one of the millions that are impacted by sleep paralysis. Knowing this, he continued drinking, trying to score with random hotties, working out, and whatever the hell else he wanted to. He would barely get any sleep while carrying on with his partying ways and loved to say, "I'll sleep when I'm dead" to anyone who asked about his constant partying.

One late August night at a beach party, Kyle offered to drive a chick back to her condo complex. He was driving her home hoping to score with her, but he was trying to be a gentleman about it. He was too drunk to drive anyway and had told her he was fine.

It's only a couple blocks, and nobody is on the streets anyway. I can't ruin this chance. It's Saturday night, and she'll probably be a lame-ass bitch wanting to go to church tomorrow anyway.

As they were nearing her complex, he turned up his hip-hop station, hoping to get her in even more of a mood. She started dancing in the car and laughing, as he paid attention to her and not the road. Her eyes were closed as she simultaneously pumped her fists in the air and bounced up and down in the passenger seat. He kept staring at her bouncing boobs, hoping to get a chance with her. When he realized that he hadn't noticed the road in what seemed like a few minutes, he looked up from her boobs and slammed on the brakes, but not before wrapping the truck's front end around an electric pole.

The crash had knocked her out, but the airbags had deployed, and her seatbelt kept her well protected. She woke up to a police officer asking her some questions, but she couldn't comprehend them yet. The paramedic put a collar around her neck and strapped her to a spine board. She started to panic, but the officer and paramedic kept reassuring her that she was in good shape considering the accident she had just been in.

"Accident?" she questioned.

"Yes, you were in a bad accident, but you are lucky to be in this great of shape," the paramedic told her.

"The truck is registered to a guy named 'Kyle.' Do you know him?" the officer asked.

"We met at a party, and he was taking me home," she said.

"Was he drinking too?" the officer asked.

She was still drunk, concussed, and confused a bit but answered as truthfully as she could, "I saw him with a drink or two, but he said he was good. Why? What's wrong?"

She tried to sit up and look but realized she was completely strapped down when the officer said, "Do you have any idea why he would flee the scene and just disappear then?"

"I honestly don't know, officer. We just met," she said in disappointment.

She was lifted into the ambulance, and the doors closed behind them as the paramedic climbed in.

CHAPTER FOUR

Maddie and Machelle walked slowly to the mysterious guest, whose arms were placed on the table around the old book. Maddie and Machelle walked closer as the guest raised an arm and extended their fingers, signaling for them to be seated. As the two young ladies obliged and got closer, they could hear the rain getting heavier and thunder rumbling in the distance.

The figure remained cloaked under the baggie hooded jacket. All they could see were the hands, which were weathered and wrinkled. Maddie and Machelle looked at each other and pulled back the older wooden chairs to be seated.

Maddie thought, *Who the hell is this person? And why the hell did Machelle bring me here to meet them?*

The hooded figure remained under the dim light and finally started to speak slowly. A high-pitched, raspy voice said, "I know what you are thinking. Who the hell is this? And why did she bring me here?"

Maddie looked puzzled and shocked as she squinted to see who this was. *Who is this? How did she read my exact thoughts?* She tried to keep her mind clear and let this mysterious person speak without having to read her mind.

The hooded figure pulled back her hood and let the sparse light reveal her face. To Maddie and Machelle's surprise, this lady looked like a regular elderly lady. She sat there with her arms still extended around the book. Her hair was straight and white, about shoulder length, and she had dark brown eyes. Surprisingly, her face didn't have many wrinkles or other imperfections.

As Maddie sat there trying not to think and have her mind read, the old lady started to speak again. She told Maddie, "We've noticed your continuous research on various religions, purgatory, and karma." Before Maddie could fully think about what we might mean, the old lady continued, "Yes, we. Our coven has been watching you for many years. You are a very passionate empath, and we can read your energy. We've been able to follow you for years, and I'll show you proof."

Maddie gave Machelle a confused look but leaned closer to the old woman.

"That businessman that you followed and confronted a few years ago, karma came and bit him in the ass. His wife caught him cheating with an intern, she called his boss, and they both got fired. The accounting firm found out he had embezzled tens of thousands of dollars. They pressed charges, and he fled. He ended up getting cornered at a rest stop in Arizona. He was taken into custody and then took his life while awaiting trial. If you don't believe me, here are the articles. I also have a picture of you confronting him that day."

Maddie and Machelle sat there with their jaws dropped. Maddie stared at the picture of her confronting this guy. She remembered that vividly. She then swapped the picture for the newspaper clippings with Machelle and read the short articles. She was happily satisfied that she and those kids had finally gotten some justice. She then cocked her head to the side to look over Machelle's shoulder at the picture as she tried to formulate questions for the old woman.

The lady let Maddie ask the questions she could read in her mind aloud so Machelle could hear them before she answered Maddie. "Did you take that picture? Who is this we, and how many of you are there? What are these bars on a meter next to him and me? Exactly how long have you been following me? Why me? Why are you telling me this stuff now? Where did you come from? Is this ominous thunderstorm your doing? What is this book?"

Machelle looked at Maddie with wide eyes and could see her

emotions and excitement all at once. At this point Maddie was leaning forward with intrigue, and the old lady didn't even move. She just studied Maddie as she asked question after question. They were all valid questions, and Machelle wanted the same answers as Maddie. She hadn't seen Maddie show such excitement before and definitely had never heard her talk this much.

The lady let Maddie cool down and relax back in her chair before she spoke. As Maddie cooled down, Machelle and the lady looked at her with wide eyes. The lady and Machelle knew Maddie was not this excitable and were taken aback by it. Machelle slowly turned her attention back to the lady, anticipating the answers to Maddie's line of questions.

The old lady looked out the window as lightning cracked within a mile of the window with instant thunder. As the nearby thunderstorm carried on, she began to speak. "Yes, this storm is me. It's my way of keeping pesky people away from us. It's like my own sound machine," she said with a high-pitched chuckle.

She continued. "My name is Ethel, by the way. I'm part of a coven that goes back to before the Great Roman Empire. In fact, those curses that supposedly surround sarcophagi are real. We placed curses on the sarcophagi as a deterrent to let those in them have eternal rest. As for how many of us there are, I can't discuss numbers. After the Salem Witch Trials, we don't discuss numbers. Only a few really know. We can't be compromised like that again. As for you, yes, I took that picture of you. I was assigned to this region, and I could feel your energy early on. I could tell that you are an empath. You are one for justice. You also seem to be quite reserved."

Machelle chuckled loudly at that notion, breaking some of the seriousness. Machelle felt bad about her chuckle killing the mood but couldn't help herself. That made Maddie smile.

Ethel continued, "With you being quite reserved, we appreciate that. It helps ensure our secret isn't leaked again." As she said it, she gave Machelle a glare that sent chills through her as a bolt of lightning cracked nearby.

Ethel kept answering Maddie's questions, "Yours and Machelle's ongoing research of karma and purgatory for some time now has gotten our attention, and we've had many discussions about your reasons for researching—if you both are worthy of even this conversation." She paused to see their faces and to read their shocked expressions. A few more flashes of lightning and loud cracks of thunder roared around them.

Ethel continued, "The lines you see on the photograph next to you are measurements of karma. We possess a power that allows us to read people's energy levels and see their karma levels. Think of it as being like a gas tank. The fuller the tank, the better the karma. The emptier the tank, the worse the karma. See his levels here? He was about ten percent from being empty. Your levels have been some of the highest we have ever seen. This is why when you all moved out this way, your mom got a great job and was able to do well for your family. His levels were low by this point, and within six months, he met his downfall."

"Wait. How long have you been following me?" Machelle asked Ethel.

"When your path merged with Maddie's. That's when," Ethel responded.

This intrigued Maddie and Machelle to the point that their jaws hung open. Machelle was the first to speak up and ask, "So, wait. You can look at anyone and see a karma meter? Like a freaking video game with the character's remaining life span?"

"Yes. If that's how you want to put it. Here, let me take a picture of you two now, and I'll show you how it works," Ethel exclaimed before reaching into her shoulder bag hidden behind her on the old wooden chair. She pulled out a Polaroid camera and snapped a picture of the eager and still-shocked young ladies. The rain remained heavy while the picture slowly developed, the lightning and thunder cracking around them. After a few minutes of the purity from the sounds of the storm, the Polaroid was ready, and Ethel slid it across the table to the eagerly waiting girls.

They were stunned to see their karma levels.

"Why can't I see Machelle's level?" Maddie asked.

"Is this something that you can see all the time? Or is it like a job with a work cell phone, and you can just turn it on and off?" Machelle chimed in.

Ethel said, "You each can only see your own karma level on these photos. I can see both of them, but I did it this way so you can't judge each other. Even though your levels are mostly full, I still didn't want any judgments. It is something that we can turn on and off, thank goodness. Otherwise, that would be exhausting. I want you two to remain focused on the bigger picture. I allow you to see what I want you to see. Now look back at the photo."

"One more quick question. How do you see it if you don't have some device or a photo? Do you have special contact lenses or what?" Machelle eagerly asked.

"No, it's just something within our powers. We don't need any special devices. It just comes with being in the coven. To easily explain, it's like a heads-up display in an airplane. You flip it down, and you can see things the naked eye can't. Then you flip it up, and you see what everyone else sees," Ethel explained. "Only we don't have to flip anything. We just imagine that we can see the karma levels in our field of vision, and then we can. I only took a photo so I could show you your levels."

The karma levels disappeared, and the image soon followed. Ethel continued, "We would like to invite you both to join our coven. Should you accept the invitation, you both will begin to have and utilize powers beyond your comprehension—of course, under direct supervision and on a probationary status. Maddie and Machelle, you both are here today for a reason. You both have been on a quest for answers that few could even fathom. Should either of you not accept, this will be wiped from your memory, and you'll go about your day as normal. Should you accept and this information gets leaked, we will erase all evidence except your memory, and you'll be treated as mentally insane because no one will believe you. Now, before we get to the book, what is your idea of purgatory?"

⬦————————————⬦

Kyle slowly regained consciousness. As he opened his eyes, he squinted to try and see in the darkness. He closed his eyelids again, rolled his eyes around, and reopened them but couldn't see anything. He had found himself in pure darkness. He tried to move and find a light source of some kind.

If I can find a light switch or my cell phone, I can find my way out of this closet or whatever the fuck I'm in. Then I'll find out if Chad or Brad did this to me. I swear to fucking Christ, I'll beat the living fuck out of whoever put me in here!

As he started to try to move, he realized he was completely immobile. *Ah, shit! Not this sleep paralysis bullshit again! Come on! Come get me motherfucker! You couldn't get me all these times before! You won't get me now!*

He kept trying to fight the imaginary weight that had completely paralyzed him. He tried everything—kicking, punching, crawling, running, jumping, and even doing backflips. In doing so, he tried to reach for his hat but couldn't. He tried to move his scalp to feel if his hair was out of place but couldn't.

He grew enraged. *I'm really going to beat the shit out of someone now!* He thought back to when his buddy Jake had gotten his face beat in for messing with his hat, hair, and his chance with Marissa that June night, and how that was nothing compared to the beating someone was going to get for this.

All of a sudden, a mirror with a light surrounding the glass appeared seemingly out of nowhere. Kyle looked at his face—no deformities. Phew! But as his eyes moved up to his hair and where his hat would be, he started panicking. His hair was thinned out with a receding hairline. In the mirror he saw a reflection of Marissa over his shoulder, pointing and laughing at him.

He could hear her say, "I don't want to be with someone with bad hair like that. What other bad genes do you have, small dick syndrome? No wonder you're always wearing a hat. Eww, I'm telling all my girlfriends."

Shocked and stuttering, he said, "I swear my hair isn't like this. I wear the hat to support my buddy's brewery. I swear I'm not compensating. Here, I'll show you."

He couldn't move his body, and he looked down to try to move and show her that he wasn't compensating. When he looked back up at the mirror, it was full of good-looking women who pointed and laughed at him. His face turned red with embarrassment and anger. Kyle was more pissed than he could ever dream of being. He closed his eyes, hoping it would go away. He couldn't move his arms to take the mirror and throw it away from his sight. He couldn't run. He couldn't do anything but close his eyes, but the laughter and torment continued. He couldn't even put his fingers in his ears to stop the barrage of laughter and snarky comments.

He was in agony. He wanted it to end. He pleaded, "Please make this stop! Please wake me up from this nightmare. This isn't real. It can't be real. I have a full head of hair. I was just at a beach party. I know I did my hair, and it was perfect before I left. Please, someone help me."

He closed his eyes in defeat and let the barrage of laughter and hate beat in his ears and brain. He finally gave in and was defeated. He would have to ride this nightmare out. It had to be a nightmare because Brad and Chad couldn't pull this off. They were pranksters but not of this level. Kyle took a slow deep breath and was suddenly plunged back into darkness.

When Kyle woke back up, he was sitting in a cold metal chair in the nude, a dim light hanging over him. He sat there, again confused as to what the hell was going on. At least there was light now. He still couldn't move anything but his head. He then heard what sounded like static in the background.

He cautiously said into the surrounding dark void, "Hello? Is someone there? Can you please help me? I don't know what you want, but I can help you with whatever you want. You might have the wrong guy. I just like to work hard and party hard. I don't owe you anything, do I? Whatever it is, we can work this out."

Then a loud booming and deep voice spoke. "Kyle Farmer! You are probably wondering why you are here. This is understandable. This is the unknown. I won't tell you where you are, how you got here, or if you can even get out. These are answers you must seek out on your own. You are the master of your destiny, and this will prove it. I have made it so you can't interrupt me or what I'm about to show you. Now sit back, watch, and make your decision on whether or not you'll be the master of your destiny or if you'll suffer for the remainder of eternity. Enjoy. I know I always do."

After the booming laughter faded, the static got louder, and then a screen appeared before Kyle in this room that seemed to be getting warmer. As Kyle sat in the cold metal chair in the hot room naked as a jaybird, he tried to wiggle to find some comfort but couldn't. The screen started to play. It felt like hours, but within just a few minutes, it seemed like his life played out before his eyes. It seemed like a flash but also like he was reliving everything. It felt so weird. Kyle felt a mix of emotions as everything played before him.

The first clip was of Kyle's mom and dad giving him a kiss when he was born. Feelings of love filled him as he watched. He felt the same love as he watched himself grow from an infant to a toddler. He was surprised to be feeling these emotions while watching this.

Where the hell am I? Is this some weird judgment day? I thought that was in the presence of God and not in a dark room with a big screen, he thought as more images passed.

He soon started seeing images of him cheating on his many girlfriends, sometimes with their own friends, bribing them not to tell his then girlfriend. Images of him stealing his buddy's weed.

Images of him using steroids in high school sports and proudly wearing medals he had cheated to obtain. Images of him wearing those medals while talking to junior athletes about hard work paying off. Images of him breaking up with a girlfriend after a round of botched Botox. Visions of him breaking up with another girlfriend as he walked into the hotel to meet with another woman.

The flashbacks were getting worse and worse as he sat there and watched. The fun and loving visions seemed like forever ago. The next was him slipping a roofie in a woman's workout drink at the gym. He had played the hero and taken her home but then took advantage of her. She didn't realize what had happened, thought he was a hero, and they had dated for a while. He never pulled the same move twice to let on any suspicions.

Before the screen stopped playing and went back to static, it played the most recent images of him driving drunk with a drunk woman in his truck. He planned to take advantage of her, and the vision showed his text to his buddy. *Brb, gonna go slam this drunk hottie. Gotta strike now. I'll be back at the beach for more. Lmk what tail you land. Chat soon bro.* He then saw himself getting in the truck and driving while impaired.

As the screen went to static, he hung his head in defeat and deep sorrow. All those people he had hurt over the twenty-eight years of his life. How many hundreds of lives? How many knew that he hurt them? How many didn't know? How could he make this right? Could he ever make this right? He sat there with his head down in shame. While he sat there in the heated room on the cold metal chair, he didn't care about his discomfort. As the static faded into the void of the darkness, the light suddenly went out and so did Kyle.

CHAPTER FIVE

Dan sat at his oak desk in his home office, repeatedly watching the eight-second video while occasionally pausing. He would zoom in and out to try and gain some clarity on who in the actual hell these three dudes were. Then he would watch and pause the second the car would disappear.

How is nearly everything blurry in the video, even when paused?

This boggled him because his phone had a 4K action-stable camera. He would go to the beach and capture his buddies in surfing competitions riding gnarly waves, and those videos came out perfect. This perplexed him.

With the video tab minimized, Dan opened an internet browser tab and started researching.

"You have seriously gotta be yanking my leg!" he said aloud in the direction of Juliet. "I try to do a basic search on disappearing cars and people. What do I get? I keep getting ads for tickets to see magicians in Las Vegas and articles on the Bermuda Triangle and UFOs."

He knew this type of search would be futile. He soon turned to videos on the internet in hopes of being sold a ticket to a magic show.

Dan sat on the computer for the better part of the night watching videos, or at least the intros. Most were folks claiming to be magicians, but it was all the same staged bullshit. It was definitely not like anything he had seen. He went to bed and left the tabs open on his desktop to come back to later.

Dan and Juliet woke up late the next morning, after being up until the early hours as he tunneled down rabbit holes. Dan poured himself a cup of coffee while he fed Juliet and let her out for her morning bathroom routine. He stood at the counter over his steamy coffee, watching Juliet but having flashbacks to the days before. The vision kept playing over and over in his mind, like a DVD on repeat.

The eight-second clip played endlessly in his mind. He stood there, wide-eyed, staring into seemingly nothing but the emptiness of space. Juliet coming in and licking his leg brought him back out of it. Minutes had passed, and his coffee was cool enough to sip and get some caffeine in him before he approached the situation again.

Holy shit, do I need a lot of coffee before I think through this crazy bullshit again? My stupid fucking dreams didn't help any last night! I dreamed about drowning! My one and only freaking fear. What the hell, brain? Couldn't think of anything else to dream about? Maybe I should mix an energy drink with this coffee. That'll wake you up, you stupid brain!

After he finished one mega mug of coffee, he poured another and headed to the computer. As he walked closer to his desk in the office, he was taken aback. He stopped dead in his tracks and looked around the whole desk and office. He stood a few feet shy of the entrance into his office and stared at the computer, barely noticing the weight of his big coffee mug pulling on his tendons and ligaments throughout his arm and hand.

He adjusted the coffee mug and continued to stare into his office. He began to slowly walk again, but as he got closer, his eyes got wider. He finally got to the desk, set his coffee down, and pulled the chair back to sit down. He slowly sat down without taking his eyes off the computer screen, then took a methodical sip of his coffee, his eyes staring in disbelief.

On his screen was an email from a famous magician in Las Vegas named Maddox. Dan checked the email address for authenticity. Sure enough, it was legitimate. He opened the attachment.

"No freaking way! No freaking way! How?" he said as he ran his fingers through his hair. "Seriously? Roundtrip airfare, car service to and from the airports, hotel room at the hotel the magician does shows at, a ticket to the show, and a backstage pass?" This can't be right.

He minimized the attachment tab and reread the email, "Dan, I noticed you were searching about vehicles and people disappearing. I want you to come out and see a show so we can talk more. If you don't believe me, click open the next email and link. I'll prove to you that I'm really sending you these emails and that I want you to come talk with me after a show."

He clicked out of that email and opened the next message. When he opened the attachment, he was shocked to see this magician watching the same video that was *only* on *his* computer. Dan shut his computer down immediately.

This can't be real! He pushed himself back away from the desk and held his mega mug of coffee while he sat there, completely startled. He slowly approached his desktop tower to turn it back on.

"This is some weird sci-fi shit!" he said as he pressed the power button to start up the computer again.

While the computer was turning back on, Dan purposely dumped hot coffee on himself to make sure he was still part of the spinning earth. He got up to go to the bathroom and wiped his legs off from the coffee. He then went back to find another email and attachment. The attachment was a video of Dan watching the magician watching his video and Dan turning off the computer.

In some weird defeat, Dan opened the original email to review it again and figure out how to let him know he would accept the invitation and go to meet and talk. Dan began typing a reply. "Good morning. Thank you for the offer. It took me a few minutes to see if you are real and some Nigerian Prince hacker is not pranking me. I hope we can discuss what I witnessed at our meeting. I'm still confused by all of this, how you know about my video, and even why you are interested in me. I hope you get this and know that I accept your invitation."

As soon as he finished typing and moved the cursor over to click send, he paused for a second and reread what he just typed. Just then he heard the familiar noise of his printer warming up.

⋄————————⋄

"Flight 2672 from Grand Rapids to Minneapolis is now in final boarding. Boarding *all* passengers and *all* rows. Again, flight 2672 to Minneapolis is in final boarding. Welcoming *all* rows and *all* passengers. Make your way to gate five. Doors close in ten minutes."

Oh shit! I don't have time to grab a coffee before boarding. These are some freaking early times for flights. How do people do this so often? AJ thought as she put back on her low-cut flat shoes at the security checkpoint. She hurried through the terminal and made it to gate five with three minutes to spare.

As she sat down in her window seat three-quarters of the way back in the plane, she pulled out the printouts of her confirmation numbers, locations of the hotels, and other possible haunted locations. She hoped to do some reading on this flight, explore a bit of Minneapolis during her four-hour layover, and then sleep on the longer flight from Minneapolis to Portland, Oregon. It was a good plan, but she knew her excitement level for venturing out and finally exploring the supernatural might prevent any real rest.

As the small commuter airplane powered down the runway and climbed into the goldfish-orange sky that was rapidly turning blue, AJ opened her window shade to get some natural reading light. She looked out at the partially cloudy sky that was growing smaller as the seconds ticked by. She was amazed by the plane soaring through the sky. As she was dazed by the beauty below, a sweet young flight attendant asked her if she'd like a beverage or a snack. AJ asked for a coffee and a cookie to accompany it.

She pulled her tray table down, set her freshly brewed coffee down, and opened her binder of materials to read. The first bit of information was for her first stop, Minneapolis. There, she wanted to ride a roller coaster in the middle of the Mall of America. That had always fascinated her. What better location to have some food and fun, all while being just a few feet away from shopping?

She finished her coffee and cookie just as the aircraft slowed down slightly. "We've begun our initial descent into the Minneapolis area. The current weather is seventy-five degrees and mostly cloudy. We thank you for flying with us this morning. We anticipate some choppy air on approach. We'll have you on the ground in about twenty minutes. Stacey, if you wouldn't mind preparing the cabin for arrival now, we'd greatly appreciate it."

Twenty minutes? That's plenty of time to read more about this mall and where I'll be staying tonight.

As she read more about the mall, the more excited she got. So much variety but not so much time. She'd have to get a few gifts for her folks while there, but she wouldn't have much time between landing, leaving the airport, transportation to and from, getting through security, and getting back to whatever gate. She was willing to risk it, though.

AJ's adventures to the mall turned out to be fruitful. She rode the coaster as soon as it opened. She had an early lunch, rode the coaster again, and then did some much-needed and deserved shopping. This helped her relax and brought a calming happiness to her. She completely forgot about school, grades, and working extra shifts. In fact, she was glad she had worked some extra shifts to be able to do this. As she loaded into the cab back to the airport, she was sad to leave but happy about her short time there.

As the flight from Minneapolis to Portland was barreling down the runway, AJ watched out her window in a relaxed mindset. *I hope to take Ma and Pa back here one day. It would be nice to treat them to such an amazing trip one day—maybe when Detroit plays Minnesota for a series. Dad would love to see Detroit play in another stadium one day, and Mom and I can go shopping. Then, I could catch a game with Pa. Ahhh, that would be nice.*

"The captain has indicated that we are in our final descent into Portland International Airport. Please ensure that your tray tables are locked and stowed, your carry-ons are stowed in the overhead storage or under the seat in front of you, your seats are upright, and your seatbelts are fastened low and tight across your lap. Our cabin crew is coming through to collect any trash or unused items at this time. We will be landing shortly. Thank you for flying with us today, and we wish you a pleasant stay in the Portland area or wherever you may be off to today," one of the flight attendants said over the PA.

This woke AJ up out of a dead sleep. She quickly gathered her folder and stapled documents that were spread out on her lap, the tray table, and the floor. She neatly put them back in the folder in a rush, although out of order. She put the tray table and her seat back up before adjusting her seatbelt. Just as she was tightening her seatbelt, she looked out the window and caught the impressive beauty of Mt. Hood. She quickly grabbed her phone and started snapping pictures of the impressive beastly stature of the mountain. As the plane turned on final approach, she looked out the opposite window across the airplane and gazed at the beauty of the Columbia River. She was immediately filled with excitement about this trip and was overwhelmed with joy that she had picked Portland as her destination.

The plane landed, and she spent a solid fifteen minutes watching and waiting for everyone to take their sweet time getting off the plane. She was so excited that her legs shook while she waited to deplane. When she was finally off the plane, she turned and took a picture of the airplane before turning back around to navigate the gibberish of airport signs. First stop—baggage claim!

AJ grabbed her bag from the carrousel and headed to a set of empty chairs by the door labeled *Ground Transportation and Rideshare*. She set her backpack down to retrieve the folder with the hotel information, then opened up her rideshare app and put in the address. The app indicated five minutes for pickup. She headed to the kiosk and grabbed a quick sandwich and water before her ride arrived.

The driver pulled up, honked, and waved at AJ as she waved her phone at him. He jumped out to help with her bags and did a quick introduction to ensure she was the person he was supposed to be picking up. They both hopped into the black sedan, and he opened up the map.

He looked into the rearview mirror with confused eyes. "To the *Old Portland Inn*?" he asked.

"That's correct. My first time here—gonna be a great trip!" AJ said with bold excitement.

"You know that place is haunted, right? Like, it's in the top twenty-five haunted hotels in North America," the driver continued.

"Yes, I know. I did my research," AJ said as she looked down at her phone to text her parents to let them know she had made it into Portland safely. She also wanted to let them know the rideshare driver's name and license plate number for her safety.

AJ was taking in the beauty of the surrounding scenery as the driver took her to the Old Portland Inn south of the city. She was glued to the window, hanging on to every second of the journey to the hotel. She was even more stunned when they pulled into a big turnaround that looked like it was used for limos.

The hotel looked like a billionaire's mansion, just really old. AJ could feel an energy of pain and uncertainty. She had sudden feelings of unfinished business, among a slew of other unexplainable sensations. She was still really excited but now nervous to be there. She gathered her bags and turned to thank her driver, but he was already back in the sedan and heading out of the drive before she could.

She proceeded to head into the check-in area. She was stunned by the dual curved marble staircases and the spiral chandelier. She studied the incredible old paintings in oak frames. She was studying a painting and slowly walking when she stopped and turned to the check-in desk. A Goth-looking twenty-something-year-old woman appeared.

"Checking in?" she asked in a deadpan voice.

"Um, yeah. For six nights. Here's my ID and card that I paid the reservation with," AJ responsibly replied.

"Six nights. Prepaid. We just hold an incidental charge of one hundred dollars that will be deposited back onto the card after your checkout. Room number one-ten. Breakfast is from seven to ten daily. To get to your room, go between the staircases and keep going. It'll be halfway down the hall on your left," the receptionist said.

"Awesome! Thanks!" AJ said as she turned to head to the staircases.

AJ took in all the scenery as she walked through the lobby and up the stairs. The hallway had more paintings. Some were great, and some seemed odd, but who was she to judge? This was her first time on the West Coast. As she was looking at all of the paintings in the hallway, she realized she had forgotten to look for room numbers and had passed her room. She unlocked the door and went in.

AJ was impressed by the room and just how much space it had. The view looking out at the city was fantastic. She left the blinds open and only used the sheet-like curtain to keep most of the light out. She wanted to fall asleep watching planes landing and taking off while looking at the downtown skyline. As she lay there enjoying the scenery, she fell asleep watching it all. To be fair, it was late back home, and she was exhausted from traveling all day.

AJ woke up the next morning to her parents calling to see if she was okay. She answered and told them how amazing it was there and how she had fallen asleep watching the city life from a distance. They chuckled and passed off their nervous laughter as excitement for their baby's adventures. AJ hurried them off the phone to shower and get a quick breakfast before heading out on her local adventures.

AJ stood in the big turnaround drive as she looked at her map app while finishing her coffee. She discarded the waste and began walking down the driveway. Her walk was set to be fifteen minutes.

AJ began to walk faster as she noticed the late morning could be bringing rain to the area.

Shit! I didn't bring a raincoat with me on this walk, or an umbrella! If I hurry, I can beat this storm, she thought as she picked up the pace.

From the moment she noticed the clouds rolling in until she walked up to the building should have been eleven minutes, according to the map app. She played a little game and timed herself down to eight minutes. She was thrilled with herself, especially seeing as the storm was just about to open up. She walked under the awning and turned around to see the clouds start a fast, light rain. She turned back and read the sign as she grabbed the handle to open the door. She opened the door to Used Books Plus and walked in as thunder cracked and roared nearby.

Maddie and Machelle stood side by side, about an arm's distance apart. Ethel stood in front of them with the old book opened to a page toward the end. They stood in the dim light with their right hands raised, as if swearing under oath. The thunder, lightning, rain, and winds had picked up dramatically as Ethel read the girls their oaths and described the terms of their coven's probationary phase.

"So, do we get cool capes and pointy hats?" Machelle excitably asked.

Ethel chuckled. "No, those were of the old times, and we are only portrayed that way on screen nowadays. We, in fact, *won't* be dressing you ladies up in anything funny that would make you stand out and have people ask questions. We like you to look and act normal—like you have no special abilities."

"How long is our probationary phase? Like six months?" asked Maddie.

"There is no real timeline—just a checklist and us observing you. Once we feel you are ready, you'll individually be fully sworn in," Ethel answered solemnly.

"What are we allowed to do while being observed during our probationary phase?" Maddie asked.

Ethel responded in a serious and stern voice. "You can observe people's energy levels and read their karma levels. You can transfer between the world of the living and purgatory. That has to be at times when you absolutely know you won't be seen or missed. While in purgatory, you'll be placed on a judge's panel. You'll be observing people as they are in the hellish limbo phase of purgatory. We do this so you understand the implications of sending someone to purgatory. It's not pretty, and we want you to see how damning it can be on the soul before we give you full powers. While on the panel, you'll have souls in your hands, and we have a panel to ensure that it's just and fair. You'll be deciding whether souls will be sent to hell, heaven, or back to the living world. Every decision has serious ramifications and is irreversible."

Maddie and Machelle looked at each other wide-eyed and stoic. This was a huge task that they had just accepted.

Machelle carefully asked Ethel, "Can we send anyone to purgatory while in the probationary phase?"

Ethel seriously looked at each of the girls back and forth as she said, "The only time one of you can send someone into purgatory while on probation is if you catch them red-handed harming an innocent life. Something like abusing the elderly, the disabled, a child, an unconscious person, or an animal. We investigate every time a probationary coven member sends someone to purgatory. If they abuse their powers or do it without absolute certainty, they are stripped of their powers and will pay the price. So, make sure that you do it with one-hundred-percent certainty. I suspect that after you have been on a few panels, you'll want that certainty."

The two continued to stare at Ethel with their stunned wide eyes. Ethel broke their stares by closing the book loudly and said, "Well, if you have no more questions, I have to get going. I have a great area to cover, but I am grateful to have you two aboard. I feel really good about having you with us."

Machelle asked, "When do we start our first panel?"

"Soon. I'll send a blinking glimmer in the right corner of your vision. That will be my beacon to you that it's time to transfer to purgatory. Just silently say that you are ready, and you'll be transformed from the realm of the living to the great beyond."

The storm was getting lighter, and the bookstore was gaining more natural light. Maddie and Machelle excitedly looked first at each other, then at Ethel, and then back at each other. When their eyes locked for the second time, Ethel sent a glimmer as a test. The girls excitedly saw the glimmer, and each then silently said, "I'm ready."

CHAPTER SIX

AJ opened the door as the rain started getting slightly heavier and the winds picked up. AJ looked left and then right, searching for a heavy rug or mat to wipe her low-cut hiking boots. As she was wiping the light mud and leaves from her boots, she glanced to the left at the counter where Machelle sorted through a stack of books.

From what AJ could see of Machelle, she appeared to be about five and a half feet tall. Slender but lean, she had blond streaks scattered throughout her brunette hair and dark brown eyes.

Machelle looked at AJ with a long pause and smile, then said, "Welcome to Used Books Plus. Is there anything I can help you with? Are you looking for a specific book or genre? Feel free to look around, and if you need anything, just ask. I'm Machelle."

AJ nodded and said, "Thank you. If you aren't too busy, could you point me in the direction of books on hauntings and the paranormal?"

Machelle got a jolt of excitement and concern. She motioned to AJ as she said, "Follow me, and I'll take you to the area where that genre is. We have a great selection."

The two walked to the left of the entrance to an aisle with a few shelves full of books. The shelving stacks stood about six and a half feet tall, and this section was packed. AJ thanked Machelle as she gave the books a quick once over. Machelle nodded and headed toward the front desk.

"If you need anything, please let me know," she said with a side turn and a few steps as she trailed away from her new customer.

Machelle walked around the desk and looked back at where AJ was now slowly looking over the book titles. Machelle took a long look at her and tried to get a read on her. Figuring she would be there for a while, she went into the back room. Maddie and Ethel sat in the dimly lit tiny break room. They were looking at the computer and watching the security camera. They were now watching AJ through the camera.

Maddie asked Ethel, "How old is she? What is the average karma level for someone at her age? She has to be well into the ninety percental range. That is pretty impressive for someone of this age, right?"

Ethel responded, "She is nineteen, and an average nineteen-year-old female would be in the sixties. You have to think that most people that age have been surging with hormones, which could be causing a bit of a ruckus. At early college age, these young folks tend to rebel against their parents or guardians, teachings, and upbringings. They are also exploring the world and making mistakes and just learning about life overall. As we progress in the world, we understand that kids will be kids and argue with their parents and sneak out. Their karma levels drop when they do things they know are absolutely wrong to do to a fellow person or an animal like drinking and driving, drugging someone's drink, taking advantage of an intoxicated person, stealing, and fighting, among other things."

AJ got up from her kneeling position and looked around for Machelle. The three saw this on the screen, and Machelle went to see if she needed help. While she was approaching AJ, Maddie and Ethel left the back office. Ethel grabbed her shoulder bag and walked around the counter and toward the back of the store, appearing to look for a book. Maddie went to the counter and filtered through the books on the countertop.

"Is there anything I can help with?" Machelle asked.

"Are there any specific locations in this area that are known to be haunted?" AJ asked.

Machelle couldn't think of any exact locations but stated, "Here, let me find a book on the area that may have some information of the sort."

AJ responded with glee, "Thank you so much. I have done a lot of online research, but sometimes you can't trust the internet. Especially on something that isn't too tangible. It's not something like a train museum, you know?"

Machelle nodded. "Here is that book. Are there other locations that you may want to read about?" Machelle asked.

"The only things I could find anything credible about in the states are abandoned mental hospitals, abandoned hospitals, insane asylums, ancient Native American burial grounds, warships, battlefields, and anything dealing with serial killers," AJ replied with a little enthusiasm. She continued, "It's not like in Europe or in Asia, where they have haunted castles, beaches, villages, and forests."

"Welp, you're in luck. We have books in all those categories," Machelle responded as she motioned for AJ to follow her again.

They sparked up a conversation. AJ told her about how the paranormal had always intrigued her.

Maddie eavesdropped while she organized the brochures on the counters and categorized books to be reshelved.

AJ said something that hit Machelle really hard: "How long can one be in limbo and be haunting a location for so long? Wouldn't they eventually move on into the afterlife? How long is limbo compared to the living's time? Am I crazy, or do some of these hauntings last for centuries?"

Machelle was puzzled by the questions. Ethel walked into Machelle's view and looked at her with an odd smile and a raised eyebrow.

Machelle thought, *Damn! Those are some great questions. Hell if I know the answers, though.*

Ethel slowly walked away as she heard Machelle tell AJ, "Those are some really great questions. Hell, I never thought about it, but maybe these books will help you find some of those answers or lead you in the right direction."

AJ said, "Thank you. I'll take these five books. I hope they give me some answers. I'm on my two weeks off college, and I want to read more books. It's all so interesting and fun to learn about, so it's not like reading some textbook for a class that doesn't interest me."

Machelle and AJ walked to the counter to check out. Ethel walked out the door and seemed to head out. AJ chatted with Machelle for another few minutes while going through the checkout process. Maddie was done and waiting for Machelle to finish the transaction and lock up.

At this point, the storm had passed, and AJ was fine to walk back up the hill back to her hotel to read her newly acquired materials while lying in a bed in the most haunted hotel on the West Coast. AJ said she hoped to be back to get more books before heading back home in a few days.

"Maybe I'll ditch some of my toiletries and clothes so I can fit more books in my luggage," AJ said as she smiled and chuckled.

Maddie and Machelle laughed with her.

They locked up and watched AJ walk up the hill to her hotel. They began talking.

"I know we don't have much experience, but Ethel sure seemed impressed by her karma level," Machelle told Maddie as they buckled into the car.

"She sure was excited and impressed," Maddie agreed. "Why don't we take our time shopping and get some time seeing other people's karma levels."

"That sounds good to me. Anything to avoid more schoolwork," Machelle half joked.

"We have some time before my mom gets home anyway," Maddie excitably said.

"That girl had some really great questions. I mean, you don't hear about ghosts wearing modern clothing much. Is that part of purgatory? To roam a certain part of the earth watching life pass by while they are stuck. Is that a tactic still used? If so, do they—well, I guess we—drape the spirits with garb from the eighteenth century to not draw suspicion?" Machelle asked Maddie.

Maddie looked at Machelle like she was turning into a conspiracy theorist.

"Let's just go shopping, and maybe our time on the panels can answer some of those questions," Maddie said with a single raised eyebrow.

"That's fair," Machelle said in return.

After seemingly hours in the store observing everyone, they were finally ready to check out. As they walked to the car to place the groceries, Maddie began to talk about what they had just experienced, "We were in there a while. What do you think the average karma level was for what we witnessed in there?"

"I would say below fifty percent but higher than twenty-five to thirty percent," Machelle said as she closed the trunk.

"I would give it a more generous thirty-five to forty percent," Maddie exclaimed with some pausing for reflection and math estimates.

"Let's say forty and get you home with groceries before you're grounded until you're forty," Machelle said, and they both laughed.

"I don't know about you, but I am wiped out from viewing all those karma levels," Machelle said with a sigh.

"I feel the same. I'm so glad we can turn it off, though. Like Ethel told us from the beginning, if not, it would be exhausting."

"Sheesh, I'm exhausted just from walking around for that little bit today and reading the levels."

The girls pulled up to the house and were soon greeted by Mel.

"How are things at the bookstore?" Mel asked as she grabbed an arm full of groceries.

"Oh, you know. Not too busy, but still busy stuff to do. A lot of organizing, reshelving, and categorizing," Machelle said as she grabbed a few bags too.

"Any new or interesting customers?" Mel asked as she tried to keep the conversation from getting too vague and fading off.

"We had one come in today. Didn't catch her name, but she is from out of town. She joked about books and her luggage weight allotment," Machelle said with eye rolls from Maddie.

Mel sounded intrigued. "Hopefully she comes back in, and you two can talk with her some more. Did she seem like a good person?"

Maddie and Machelle furrowed their eyebrows in confusion.

"I just ask because you two never bring up anyone in particular," Mel continued.

The girls gave each other the look of wanting to end this conversation. Then they noticed a little glimmer in the upper right corner of their eyes.

"Welp, we better get going back to the store to do some inventory on some recently arrived books and some online orders," Maddie said suddenly.

"You two don't work too hard. Enjoy fun things while you're still young," Mel said as she walked them out to the car.

"Maddie won't work too hard. She never does," Machelle said with a sly grin.

"You know how volunteers are. We do just enough to not get fired," Maddie said, trying not to smile.

"Haha! Well, that wouldn't look great on a college application," Mel said as she closed the passenger-side door.

The two soon arrived back at the bookstore and went in and locked the door behind them. They walked to the back to set their stuff down in the break room and together said, "I'm ready."

AJ lay in her bed at the Old Portland Inn, skimming through the books as she talked to her parents on the phone.

"Ma, you and Pa have to visit here sometime. I haven't spent time in the city, but this outlying town is so amazing. The folks here are so nice. I'll tell you more about these girls before I head home. They are fantastic," she said, pausing for her mom's response. "Yes, it was worth my hard work. Look, Ma, I know it's getting late out there. I'll go to the bookstore tomorrow for more books and to talk with them." She stood up and stretched. "Okay. Yup. Okay. I love you too, Ma. Tell Pa that I love him."

AJ went off to bed early, as she wanted to try and keep her body on the same time as back home. She figured this would help with her transition getting back home and to class. Just as she was heading off to bed, she couldn't shake the feeling that she was being watched—but not in a creepy way. It felt more like a supernatural or paranormal manner. This excited her, as she thought the haunted hotel was about to reveal its truth and she'd get some haunted stories to tell back home. She lay in bed for half an hour, wide awake, hoping to see even a shadow move across the wall. She plugged in a camera with a big micro-SD card in it so she could film the room while she slept. Once she got the camera on and running, she dozed off.

The next morning, she woke up and headed out on her adventures with her camera. She was going to visit some burnt-out, abandoned buildings and old churches to see if she could get any feeling of paranormal activities. She ended up visiting quite a few places and had different feelings in some of the spots but couldn't see much. She continued to visit the listed haunted locations on and off over the coming days. On her last day, she went back down to Used Books Plus to see Maddie and Machelle before heading back on the night flight.

"Your bags don't weigh fifty pounds yet?" Maddie joked in a seemingly surprised manner as AJ walked into the store.

Machelle turned and looked at Maddie with a shocked face. Maddie gave her a cheeky grin.

"I just needed a few brochures to put me at an even fifty," AJ happily joked, bringing all three to a giggle.

"We left your pile of books alone. You know, just in case you came back," Machelle said with a directional head nod.

"Thank you," AJ said and followed the direction of her nod.

Maddie and Machelle soon made their way back to AJ. "So, what brings you to town? Aside from testing airline scales?" Machelle asked.

"I have always been fascinated by the paranormal. It's so intriguing. I mean, we all experience death, but no one truly knows what goes on beyond our physical earthly bodies," AJ responded.

This comment made Maddie and Machelle tense slightly and not look at each other.

"There isn't anything paranormal where you are from?" Maddie asked, hoping to bring out an answer on where she lived.

AJ sadly responded, "Nothing ever happens in Grand Rapids. It's not known for anything of the sort."

"What have you explored around here?" Machelle asked inquisitively.

"Oh, just an abandoned hospital, a former insane asylum, and a burned-out church. I always see Hollywood movies and TV series about abandoned hospitals and insane asylums being haunted. I figured a burned-out church would be a good spot, too," AJ excitedly said back to Machelle.

"Did you see or feel anything?" Maddie asked with a raised brow.

"No, nothing that I could physically see or feel. I went during daylight hours. I did set up a few cameras in each spot, though. Just to see if I could capture anything. I have some large capacity micro-SD cards that should've been able to handle the high resolution and the amount of time," AJ said with more excitement. "I mean, I wonder how long some of these places have been haunted. When does one's spirit move on? Why would their spirit be in limbo for so long?"

Maddie and Machelle looked at each other with a smirk. They knew they could answer some of those questions but couldn't because of their coven contract.

AJ saw them smile at each other and, with a shy, confused cock of her head, asked, "Why are you two smiling like that? Do you know something that I don't know?"

Maddie jumped to speak first, "We are smiling because we

have the same questions as you and are so intrigued by all these unknowns, just like you. Say, why don't we get your information, so we can stay in touch? We would love to be friends with you, and we could all talk about this kind of stuff. That way we wouldn't have to feel like we are being weirdos about our curiosity. So why do it alone and worry about being different? That's how people become friends, by having similar interests. Right Machelle?"

Machelle was quick to chime in and said, "Absolutely! That's how we became friends. Maddie came in one day, like you, looking for similar materials. We sparked up a conversation, and with a little bit of me badgering her, we became friends. I will say this, though—her brother is cute, and I already called dibs."

AJ gathered the books that she had picked out for her trip back, and they headed to the front desk. She set her books down and grabbed the pen and notepad as she jotted down her information for Maddie and Machelle. While Machelle was ringing up the books and finalizing the transaction with AJ, Maddie jotted down her information and included Machelle's for AJ.

Machelle helped walk her out and said, "Safe travels back, and we will be seeing you soon."

AJ walked back up the hill to the hotel so she could complete her late checkout and head to the airport. AJ's journey home was uneventful. She slept the entire night flight and was too tired to read or do anything else while she waited around Atlanta's International Airport. She just wanted to sleep and get some rest before starting the fall semester of her freshman year of college.

When she arrived home, she sent Maddie and Machelle a message to let them know she had made it home safely. She was excited to finally upload all of her hotel and adventure videos to skim through over the next few days. She thought that would be a great way to decompress and continue her excitement about her big adventures.

She began uploading the video footage the afternoon she arrived home. While the footage uploaded, she took a nap and waited with excitement to tell her parents about the trip. When her parents arrived home, she gave them hours of details and told them about her new friends with such excitement that her parents expressed just as much excitement for her. She then went back to her room to put on her noise-canceling headphones and start skimming over the footage. Soon after she had gotten past her passing out on her first night in Portland at the Old Portland Inn, something caught her eye.

Kyle came to again, still bound naked on a cold metal chair with his head hung in shame. A dim light slowly highlighted him in the dark abyss, gathering his attention. He suddenly had the urge to pee.

How is it that I have to pee? Where in the hell do I even go?

A urinal appeared a few feet away, and his bindings disappeared. He got up and walked to the urinal, maintaining his confusion as he looked around. He started to pee.

"What the fuck?" he screamed as what felt like fire came from his urethra. The pain was even more intensified by the feeling of razors cutting as the flaming urine exited his body. He screamed in pain, but the urge to pee hit his bladder even stronger. He tried to stop peeing, but the more he did, the more his bladder filled.

"Oh, God, why?" he wailed. "Someone, please make it stop!" He continued to beg for mercy as the urine stream went on and on.

Kyle stood at the urinal cold and naked, his feet feeling like they were encased in cement. He threw his head back in pain as the stream continued. Kyle began to cry as he tried to hold it in and ease the pain.

The booming voice screamed out, "Kyle, you beg for mercy? Did you have mercy on the women you took advantage of?"

Kyle, crying and whimpering, replied, "I'm so sorry. I have no excuses. I screwed up."

The booming voice remained silent as Kyle continued his struggle with the pain.

Kyle maintained a bowed head as he cried. "I'm so sorry! I really messed up. I'm so sorry. How can I make it right?"

Suddenly, his feet freed up, and his bladder felt relieved, the fire extinguished from his urethra. He wondered what was going to happen next, then felt like he was falling through a ceiling of a big open building. He saw walls and balconies as he tumbled through the air heading toward the ground. He was falling faster and faster. The ground approached fast. He thought it was all a bad dream and he'd wake up soon before hitting the ground. Then, splat!

He tried to move around while he lay there in excruciating pain. It felt like many bones throughout his body were broken. He wondered if he was dreaming.

If this is a dream, then why can I feel pain? If this is reality, then why isn't anyone helping me? Why isn't anyone calling me an ambulance?

With the last thought passing, he found himself in the cold metal chair again with no physical impairments or pain.

What in the actual hell is going on?

All of a sudden, he had the urge to pee again. *Agh! Not again!* he screamed in his head.

The same urinal appeared a few feet away from him again. This time he didn't get up. He tried to hold it in an attempt to avoid the pain that he assumed he was about to endure. His bladder filled up quickly, and he was lifted and pulled to the urinal. His feet were cemented in again.

Just before he started to pee, he screamed out, "What do you want from me? I know I messed up and did all those women wrong. I'm so sorry!"

The booming voice spoke again, "Are you remorseful? Do you know how many you wronged? Do you know how you altered their lives forever? Or are you just sorry because you are here now? Do you know how many of those women cry at random times throughout their lives? Do you even care to know how many future relationships you destroyed because of trust issues? Or do you only care because of the pain you are experiencing now? How about the many lifetimes of pain that you brought upon them? Are you remorseful for that?"

Kyle began fully crying as he started his next stream of extreme pain. He had never thought about those things. He just thought it was an easy score because they were intoxicated. He didn't think of the long-term effects on the women because they weren't being forced.

The booming voice spoke again, "Just because you never forced anyone doesn't mean it was consensual. Impairment doesn't mean consent!"

Kyle screamed in pain as he opened a steady flow. "I deserve this!"

He just stood there peeing away as the pain tore through his soul. But he knew he deserved it and accepted that he was to fully pay for his actions in wronging women. He stood there in pain, trying to remember the faces, locations, and names of the women he had wronged.

While standing there with his head hung low and whimpering in pain and sorrow, he heard a very unusual sound. It sounded like the slow tapping of heels on the wall above him. He thought it might be just some crackling in the speakers. He didn't think anything of it and kept peeing while crying and figuring out how to right his wrongs.

He heard the tapping getting closer. He felt his bladder finally empty, and his feet become free again. He braced for another fall, but that didn't happen. Instead, he stood there naked and cold. He kept turning and looking around, wondering what was going to happen next. He heard the tapping again. This time it seemed to be closer and louder. He franticly turned around and around but couldn't see anything but a urinal. Then he looked down. Nothing. Then he looked up.

"Oh shit!" he screamed as two giant spiders leaped at him.

"Oh shit!" he yelled again after he dodged them and took off running.

He was now running down a cement path, and the spiders

were chasing him. He felt like he was running on a treadmill. No destination was in sight, and the spiders were gaining on him. He screamed out as he looked over his shoulder and saw them leap at him again. As they neared him, he began to fall into the abyss again.

Instead of floors in a building, he saw nothing but darkness and white at the bottom.

Phew! That must be a net I can land in, and then I'll wake back up in the chair. Even better, I could wake up in my bed.

No sooner after he finished the thoughts, the whiteness grew closer, and he flailed away during his freefall. He continued down to the bottom. He calmed himself, thinking a net would catch him, and it would be all over. That soon changed as he noticed that it was not a nice, smooth polyester net that awaited his fall. It was a web.

"A web!" he yelled in surprised panic.

He noticed the two spiders had created a web and eagerly awaited his arrival. Kyle flailed even more but continued to fall faster. To his dismay, he landed in the web like a baseball into the first baseman's glove.

Kyle twirled around in the webbing and became entangled. The two spiders enjoyed watching him beg and plead to be released as he got caught further. The spiders watched him like a fresh fly in a web on a hot summer's day. After he stopped moving, they ran over, fully wrapped him up, and began stinging him with their paralytic poison.

The booming voice began speaking after the spiders stung him on many accounts, "You feel paralyzed and helpless? How do you think your victims felt? Helpless! Motionless! Do you feel that? Shed your tears. Just like they all did and still do."

Kyle began crying and continuing his remorse while he felt the pain, the shame, the agony, and the guilt. Eventually, the paralytic poison completely consumed him, and all went black again.

CHAPTER SEVEN

T hree males sat before the three panel members, each hunched over, naked, freezing, and strapped to the cold metal chair while remaining unconscious. Although they couldn't see each other, the three panel members could see each of them clearly. Each started to slowly awaken in the pitch darkness.

A faint light started to shine on each of them. Greyson came to and started to try to fight to break free. The more he fought, the more he was pulled into the chair.

"Chad! Todd! I know you two are behind this! Untie me from this chair or else!" Greyson yelled. "Ugh! I swear this stupid prank isn't funny! You can come out now and unleash me. I swear I won't beat your faces in with your limp, broken arms." He continued to struggle. "How did you two dipshits tie such good knots? You saw what I did to Timmy's little brother when he tried to prank me. You're next!"

All of a sudden, he was pulled up into the darkness, the light staying on him. He tried to scream, but the speed controlled his speech. Then he fell rapidly, the chair crashing hard into the cement, sending metal shards through his testicles, penis, and rectum. He screamed in pain, then passed out.

He awakened again, sitting in the chair but without the metal shards in his groin. Confused, he questioned where he was. *Where in the Sam Hill am I? My friends are too dumb to put together something like this. What is going on?*

A booming voice startled him, "You have no idea why you are here? You really have no account of your transgressions against your fellow people?"

"Who said that? Who's there? Is it you, Todd? I'll beat your face in if I find out it's you!" Greyson growled.

"Never mind who I am!" the voice exclaimed while Greyson felt his lips being sealed and the feeling of sutures slowly sewing his mouth together.

He panicked and tried to fight, breathing heavily. He sat in the chair, trying not to move while his eyes searched for answers.

Where the hell am I? Who could be invisible but sew my lips shut? This has to be some weirdly messed up dream. I didn't take any shrooms or acid recently, did I?

The booming voice said, "Enough is enough! You are here to pay for your transgressions. Do you realize how many people you have hurt? You have had many opportunities to make things right but keep falling back into the same routine. All you care about is yourself and getting yours. You are a user and abuser. Do you remember leaving Leann at the hospital and ghosting her after your rendezvous with her? Did you know that she became a paraplegic after that skiing accident and had to bring that guilt and shame back to her family of two kids and her husband? Do you care to know the living hell she goes through daily? Your last and final transgression was wrecking another home, all while knowingly transferring a sexually transmitted disease to that wife. Now you are here to suffer for your horrible actions. Karma has finally found you."

Greyson sat there, squinting his eyes in confusion. He still wasn't getting it. He still thought his friends were pranking him or even worse—*Oh shit! What if this is one of the husbands?*

He sat there, unable to speak or move, trying to figure out who could have him or how they had such crazy powers.

While Greyson sat there, his two friends were also fighting their introduction into purgatory. They were putting up bigger fights and blaming others, not taking any responsibility for their actions. They ended up with their mouths sewn shut too.

The three on the panel were perplexed by the men putting up such a fight before them. Most people got a grasp of what was going on fairly quickly, but a few, like the three before them, would continue to fight and not accept fault. Even though they were held motionless in the chair and couldn't move or speak, they still tried to fight.

Although the men in front of them couldn't speak, the panel could hear their thoughts, and they were not pleasant. Their thoughts were filled with curse words, pure hate, anger, threats, and even images of what they would do to whoever was pulling these "pranks" on them. The panel then cleared their thoughts and made them fall into the dark abyss, where they would tumble and fall for some time.

Greyson stopped falling through the abyss and came to rest in the chair again, a projector-like screen appearing before him. His lips were still sewn shut. The projector started rolling images of his childhood, and he was filled with happy thoughts. The images quickly fast-forwarded through his youth and on into high school. They slowed down to show him lying to his friends, getting with their girlfriends, and then breaking their hearts. The images were of the many girls he had made cry and the many friends he had screwed over while continuing his lies.

He was shown his college years. A bigger campus and being a college athlete had allowed him to cause more hurt. The images showed him lying to women in emails, social media, texts, and at bars, all while stabbing his friends in the back.

Greyson sat there, unable to speak but wondering, *Wait! Who the hell has images of all of these memories? I don't remember anyone else there during many of these times. I can understand a hidden camera on occasion. Hell, I've done that shit!* He smiled at those memories.

Images then popped up of him setting up hidden cameras to secretly film women having sex with him. And then they showed his mother going through his computer and finding those files, a look of horror on her face.

In dismay, he tried to close his eyes, but the panel pulled his eyelids into his skull, forcing him to watch his mother's cries of shame.

The panel could see his lack of remorse for all the pain he had caused. So, they showed him the images of every person he had harmed, including the women in therapy trying to deal with their abuse and the trust issues they developed as a result. He was shown the images of them crying in their therapists' offices. Session after session and boxes of tissues full of tears. He still had no remorse and became angry that someone was invading his privacy.

The panel then pulled out the big guns and showed him dropping off a woman he was having an affair with at the hospital by their ski resort after an accident on the slopes.

Again, this angered him even more because he knew no one had seen that incident. The video continued as he drove away while she was examined and told she would be a paraplegic. She was hysterical and all by herself in a hospital room. The next clip showed her calling her husband and him driving up to be with her and take her home. She was bawling her eyes out the whole drive, telling her husband of the affair and how sorry she was. There were more clips of her and her husband in marriage counseling and at church with their kids.

Greyson felt a small amount of shame for that dirtbag move but thought, *How was I to know she would be a limp-legs afterward? I just dropped her off and drove away, blocking her number after telling her never to text me. How could I know the ultimate outcome?*

He felt his mind go black, and another video appeared before him. It was of him quickly getting dressed as he heard a garage door opening. The video followed him running downstairs and out the sliding glass door, then scaling the wall behind that house. The image showed the husband going upstairs to find his wife in bed naked and then back downstairs to the sliding glass door being open. He yelled out to his wife that they were through and that she and her stuff better be out when he got back from whipping that guy's ass.

The following clip showed the man driving around in anger with a bat in hand and no seatbelt, as he was ready to jump out and find the man who had just destroyed his marriage. He had a still image from the home security camera pulled up to try and ID him. The video cut to Greyson and his two buddies in their sedan fleeing and about to crash into a white wall.

◇――――――――◇

Dan put his tray table up, as his flight into Las Vegas was in final approach. He was anxious about what awaited him on this curious adventure. He could normally sleep, even on short flights such as San Diego to Las Vegas, but what awaited him had his mind racing.

Am I really crazy for accepting an offer for a trip to Vegas by someone who hacked my computer and claims to have some crazy way of accessing everything, even my most inner thoughts? But why wouldn't I believe him? The guy could read my thoughts! Oh well, we'll see what happens. Worst-case scenario, it's a free trip to Vegas, Dan thought as he finished his coffee and handed the flight crew his empty cup.

The plane landed, and Dan grabbed his carry-on and waited while the plane slowly cleared aisle by aisle. When he exited the plane, he was tempted to play some slots in the airport while walking to the terminal exit. As he passed through the security exit, he looked around for the rideshare locations as he pulled up the apps to see time and prices.

"Dan! Over here!" He heard a voice shouting from his right.

He walked over to find an immaculately dressed gentleman holding a big tablet device with his name and a picture of him and what he was currently wearing. The photo had obviously been taken while he was still on the plane in San Diego. He stared in disbelief and complete shock. But he had no other choice but to believe.

The gentleman stood there with a stoic face and took Dan's bag with a signal for him to walk with him. They walked outside to an awaiting limo. Dan stood looking at this massive limo and thought,

This is one big-ass ride, and all for me? Even if I stretch all the way out, I could still fit another of me in here.

The gentleman opened the door and signaled Dan to get in. After Dan climbed in and began scoping it all out, his bag was carefully placed on the seat. He had his favorite drinks and snacks laid about nice and neat in the small bar area.

Okay, now this is a bit freaky! How does he know I like sushi, Reese's Cups, and Dr Pepper? Well, I guess I have to keep trusting him at this point.

Dan had often been to Vegas but never ridden in a limo. He was even more shocked when the driver passed the hotel. He was just about to click the button to talk to the driver when he heard a voice start speaking, and the screen's brightness caught his eye.

"I know you are wondering why the driver just passed the hotel. I want you to enjoy your time in the limo for a while, so we're taking you for a tour down the Strip and the historic downtown. Pop open the sunroof and soak it in. You'll be at the hotel in time to rest before the show. Enjoy, and don't worry. Oh, and you're already checked in to your room. No need to wait in line. Boris, the driver, has your key and will ensure you get all settled. I'll see you at the show tonight."

Who was Dan to argue with this? He soaked it all up—while eating eel roll sushi from the limo sunroof as they slowly cruised down the Strip. He enjoyed sushi with his favorite beverages and loved people-watching on the packed streets. He went up one side of the Strip into the historical downtown and turned around to hit up the other side of the Strip until he arrived at the hotel.

Dan got to his massive room suite and waited for his bag to make it up to him so he could enjoy the Jacuzzi bathtub with the TV in the wall. While he waited, which wasn't long, he opened the fridge and found more of his favorites, but a different variety. He was soon in the bathtub drinking ice-cold sodas and watching TV while soaking it in.

Dan was so distracted by the full-on VIP treatment that he had nearly forgotten why he was in Vegas to begin with. Then he saw a commercial come on the TV. The magician named Maddox was advertising the show set to take place in just a few hours. He kept saying lines like: "Tonight's show is one to not miss" and "Tickets are vanishing fast."

He probably uses this same commercial for every weekend show. Like those prerecorded commercials on satellite radio. Sometimes they use the same commercial for years.

Then he heard Maddox say, "This is a one-time opportunity, so don't miss it! Only tonight, August 27."

After just a few hours of arriving in iconic Las Vegas, Dan arrived at his seat and was in the third row and center of the stage at the surprisingly big theater. He kept scanning the pamphlet with the show information and looking around the theater.

The seats appeared to be all full of eagerly waiting magic fans. He noticed some folks in the balcony seats that he assumed were celebrities and other magicians.

After about twenty minutes of scanning around, the lights went out, and music began playing. Stage fog began to roll out in front of the large curtains. Lights began to flash and move around in circles.

The curtains opened, and everyone was expecting Maddox to come running out or instantly appear. But the music kept playing, and nothing happened on stage. Dan noticed a square cutout in the stage and thought Maddox would surely come popping up out of center stage like an '80s rock star shooting up from the stage.

The music kept playing, and everyone looked around for the famous magician. Then someone noticed something slowly coming down from the ceiling. Maddox was slowly floating down on a square cutout from the center balcony to the stage. Dan studied to see if any cables were holding him. He saw none.

Dan watched the fit magician, who stood about five feet nine inches with slicked-back black hair, float onto the stage to start his show. Dan was thoroughly impressed with his performance.

He was still doubtful about everything but tried to enjoy the show. He didn't think he could thoroughly enjoy the show like everyone around him because he still had so many questions about why he was there and what Maddox knew about him.

About a third of the way into the show, Maddox started to engage the crowd. He said, "I'm going to pick out a volunteer. Someone that I have never met before. Who all here is at your first Vegas show? Raise your hands."

After scanning and being impressed by the number of raised hands, he continued. "Okay. Now, who here, by a show of hands, is this your first ever magic show?"

Surprised by nearly seeing the same number of hands, he said, "Okay. Okay. So now, I want. Umm. Ugh. You. Over there. In the third row."

The spotlight swiveled and blinded Dan, but he could see Maddox pointing at him and signaling him to come up on stage.

"Yeah, you. You're blinded by the light, not by science. Come on up," Maddox teased.

The crowd cheered, and Dan got up and walked up on stage.

"Look at the crowd and tell them if we have ever met before," Maddox instructed Dan.

Dan started to talk to the audience without the microphone. Maddox slyly put the microphone under Dan's chin so the crowd could hear with the sound system.

"Yes, that is correct. We have never met before," Dan said in a truthful and bold statement.

"Can you confirm for the lovely audience here that no wires or special devices are attached to me?" Maddox asked Dan.

Dan, a natural smart-ass, didn't just do a quick glance. Instead, he started swiping the air above Maddox and pretending to strip-search him. The crowd laughed at his antics.

"Be careful, or you may become my apprentice," Maddox said, facing the crowd with a sly grin.

Maddox looked at Dan and then at the crowd before saying, "And for my next act, I'll make my new friend disappear. He will reappear somewhere within this theater. Just to double confirm, there are no wires or devices."

Dan looked very puzzled and scared, but Maddox said something that didn't make Dan any more comfortable. Maddox said, "Don't worry, I won't make you permanently disappear. I'm not the mob—or a politician."

The crowd chuckled as Dan laughed nervously.

With that, Maddox took a few steps back and looked at Dan and then the crowd. Then Dan disappeared.

◇————————————◇

Dan was sitting on a detached balcony that brought him back to the stage. Maddox had performed a few other tricks while Dan was up in the balcony watching.

When Dan got out of the flying balcony, he stood on stage with Maddox and began explaining to the crowd. "It was like being in a fast time warp. Like in a Hollywood sci-fi movie. It was black at first, then lots of colors. Then black again. Then poof. On the balcony. No motion sickness or lightheadedness. Nothing. Amazing."

Maddox thanked him and told him to wait backstage, as he had some special gifts to reward him for his participation.

Dan watched the rest of the massive performance from the side of the stage. In the show's last act, Maddox announced that he would make another random person disappear. This captured Dan's attention because he figured it was nearing the finale, and he was intrigued as to how Maddox would pull off this disappearing act and bring the man back.

Maddox brought the man on stage and had him also explain that they had never met and that he had no cables or wires attached to him. Maddox looked at the man and the crowd. The lights went out, and there was a flash as the volunteer disappeared. The lights stayed dark and slowly lightened back up to signal the end of the show.

With a wave and a bow from Maddox, he ran off stage. A screen appeared and showed him now walking through his hotel's casino, heading to his room. He gave a wave to the camera and shouted his thanks to Maddox. He had beaten the crowd out and was already back enjoying the night.

Maddox quickly met with Dan off-stage. The magician told him, "Hang out and make yourself at home while I go about and mingle and meet with everyone that has backstage access."

Dan enjoyed all of the gourmet food and fancy drinks that he could, some of which were so fancy that he couldn't even pronounce it. After what seemed like two hours, Maddox came over to Dan. By then, the whole backstage area was clear. Maddox suggested they go for a ride in his limo to talk in a private setting.

It was just before midnight on that August 27 Saturday. Dan and Maddox climbed into the waiting limo. Maddox made some more refreshments and started the TV screen.

As he did this, he said, "I know you think that you are crazy for being here and trusting me. I would sure as hell be thinking the same thing too."

Dan nodded as he took a sip of the sweet and strong drink.

Maddox continued, "You see, Dan, what you witnessed is something that no one is supposed to ever see—a car with three dudes in it just disappearing before your very eyes."

This guy is jumping right on into the topic here, Dan thought, nearly out loud.

"That's just bad craftsmanship on someone's part. I'll have to investigate further." Maddox said seemingly to himself but loud enough for Dan to hear and question more.

"Bad craftsmanship?" Dan questioned aloud, with a puzzled face.

"Yeah, we typically make people disappear when no one else is around. Because if not, then that leaves doors open for questioning. Especially in the case that they don't return."

"Um, what in the hell are you talking about? I think I either need more of that drink or to sober up right quick to continue this conversation," Dan said as he held out his glass.

"You see, Dan," Maddox started as he crossed one leg over the other and sipped from his drink. "We are supposed to make really bad people disappear when no one is around to make sure there are no witnesses and no trails."

Dan was intrigued but nervous about being alone with someone who could read his thoughts and make people disappear. He made himself a stronger drink and stared inquisitively at Maddox so he could continue.

"We like to make them disappear in areas and times where they can possibly reappear. We do this when they are in bed, hiking, in the bathroom, on long drives, or something along those lines. But alone. These are bad people who deserve to go away," Maddox told Dan.

"Go away where? And *possibly* come back? This is crazy," Dan said, feeling the alcohol relax him a bit.

"Think of driving to Vegas or Phoenix in the middle of the night on a weekday. How many miles can you drive without seeing another car? Five or more, right? We can just have someone disappear on a stretch like that and then later possibly reappear like nothing happened," Maddox exclaimed excitably.

"But, who is *we*, and where do the people go for such a short amount of time just to possibly reappear? Also, if they are so bad, then how come they could even come back at all?" Dan felt the liquid courage hit his liver and brain as he asked these questions excitedly.

"I'm a part of an organization tasked with finding people who do evil unto their fellow man—and animals—and making sure they get punished for their crimes."

Dan continued. "How do you differentiate between mental-health-driven crimes, crimes of necessity, crimes of passion, and pure evil?"

"My organization is made up of panels and teams that work together to assess people's karma levels. And we can go back into their lives to see if they were victims of abuse or trauma. Then we can read their energy and can scan them medically and chemically. This helps us from wrongfully punishing someone. If you look at a lot of crimes, they are committed by those with mental health issues, substance abuse, crimes of necessity, or they are victims themselves of prior trauma. Those situations are left in the hands of the professionals here within our land of the living. We only deal with the purely evil doers," Maddox exclaimed.

Maddox paused for a moment before continuing. "I also can't explain the *we* part of it to you unless we feel you could be one of us and handle such information. The *where* aspect is purgatory. We send bad people into purgatory. We can tell who is good, bad, and really bad. Once someone reaches a certain level, they are sent to purgatory and are punished for their transgressions. I say, 'possibly come back' because some do learn their lesson, and their souls are truly remorseful for their bad acts against their fellow humans and animals," Maddox told Dan in a lengthy speech between drinks.

"So wa-wa-wait. Purgatory is real? I thought that was a religious myth to keep people from doing bad things. What about those that don't come out of it? What happens to them?" Dan asked with a solemn face.

"Well, Dan. Like life, purgatory has a few options. One is learning your lesson, being remorseful, and possibly returning to the land of the living. Other options are staying in purgatory for some time and then going to hell, or staying for a short time and then going to hell. Either way, one has to pay for their horrible atrocities. Folks who die from other causes will visit their own versions of purgatory. We still oversee that, but it's different. I can explain that later," Maddox said with a very serious face.

"Oh wow," was all Dan could muster in response to Maddox. He took another long swig of his drink. "Back to the whole disappearing thing. So, does the car typically disappear with the person or people?" Dan asked.

Maddox responded as he finished a drink, "No, that's why this particular case was a case of bad craftsmanship. What we usually do is cause the vehicle to have mechanical issues. That way, the driver will pull off the road safely. Then they disappear. That way, it looks like they were picked up or went off walking for assistance. We also do it this way just in case they do return. It's easier and safer all around."

Maddox opened the sunroof and made two more drinks for himself and Dan. They poked their heads up from the sunroof and drank while cruising the famous Las Vegas Strip. The flashing bright lights, taxi horns beeping, street-side boom boxes thumping, crowds conversing and laughing, and cars roaring filled the air around them as the two drank and talked.

As they doubled back down the Strip, they sat back down in the limo, and the TV started repeatedly playing the eight-second video. Dan couldn't believe that he was in the limo with someone who could do that to someone. He was even more amazed at his new knowledge about it all. He sat there and wondered what kind of literal hell those three guys were going through at that very moment. He wondered, forgetting that Maddox could read his thoughts, *What shit did they do to all three land in purgatory?*

"You want to see where those three dudes are now? What hell they are living in? We can go. I can take you there," Maddox said with the utmost excitement.

"Wait! What the hell? I'm not a bad person! Why should I go to purgatory?" Dan questioned in pure fear.

"Ha! No, I meant in a purely educational sense. You already know so much. I can either show you or just clear your mind," Maddox said matter-of-factly.

Dan thought about it for a few moments. He took his drink back up to enjoy the Strip's sights, sounds, and smells one more time before either having his mind cleared of it all or venturing into purgatory. Maddox sat and patiently waited for him.

When Dan came back down, he said, "Well, I'm already this far and am really intrigued by it all. So, pardon the pun, but what the hell! Let's do it!"

Maddox smiled, closed the sunroof, and set down his glass. They disappeared into the night.

◇————————◇

Maddox and Dan entered from a room to a table where three judges sat. They walked up behind the table and viewed chambers containing those in their purgatory cells. The cells could morph into chambers, hallways, or whatever the panel saw fit for each individual's version of purgatory. No individual could see that another was in the same situation; they didn't even know that there were others there at all. Each thought that they were in there alone. But with so much horribleness in the world, they were not alone—purgatory was pretty full.

The three judges turned to their guests. Ethel greeted her friend Maddox with a warm, welcoming hug. They began making small talk before realizing that each had unfamiliar company with them.

Maddox went first. "Dan, this is Ethel. Ethel, Dan. Dan witnessed the three guys in the sedan disappearing in San Diego a few nights ago."

Ethel introduced her company, "Dan, Maddox, this is Maddie and Machelle. Ladies, please meet my longtime friend Maddox and his guest Dan."

They all shook hands. Maddie and Machelle continued their duties as Ethel and Maddox showed Dan around and gave him the full rundown of what was happening.

Ethel told Dan, "These three here are the ones you witnessed disappearing. They have a track record of being horrible humans. They still are not getting the hint, either. Each one of them thinks they are being pranked and will not accept any fault for their actions. It's not looking too promising for them. We will soon ramp up the heat and see if they feel any remorse. Even the slightest."

Dan was intrigued and responded to Ethel, "I would love to stay and see more of the process—if you all don't mind. I watched these douchebags disappear, so I kinda want to see it through."

"Absolutely. We would love to have you see what's going on. With these three, they aren't getting it, so we need to crank it up a few gears. Obviously, anyone on the other side of the table is here and needs to pay, but some are remorseful and can work through it. Some, like these three, blame others and make threats. Then, we have to increase the pressure," Ethel explained.

Dan sat down next to Ethel at the end of the table. He watched as two of the three screamed threats until their mouths were sewn shut again. Dan was drawn in at this point and on the edge of his seat. He was even more fascinated by the sound of their thoughts coming through and how atrocious they were. The panel wasted no time and pressed a button, clearing them of their purgatory cells and sending them into pure blackness to await their fate.

Dan was hooked!

Greyson was hunched over and unconscious, naked again on his cold metal chair. He woke up to a dim light shining on him. As he awakened, a bar scene appeared before him. The bar to his left and right was full of ideal-looking females. He thought maybe his luck had turned.

He got out of his chair and made his way over to the bar. He ordered a drink and began trying to make conversation with a woman near him. She turned her shoulder, so he tried turning to his left. She turned her shoulder to him too. Confused, he walked down the bar to try to talk to other women. They scoffed at him and snickered at his approaches.

Confused even more, he walked down the bar to try and get the bartender's attention. The bartender paid him no mind and started making out with one of the women. That displeased Greyson. He tried more advances, but the laughs got stronger and more frequent. Then he noticed all the women running for the door.

He thought, *Their loss. Dumb bitches!*

He turned back to the bartender to see if his drink was ready.

Hot women get their drinks before anyone else. I don't blame the bartender, but it still sucks for everyone else. They could be drunk by the time I'd even get one beer, he continued in thought as he looked around for the bartender.

Just as he noticed no one was around the bar, he heard the familiar sound of crackling wood in a fire.

Where is everyone, and why did someone start a bonfire?

To his dismay, there was no bonfire. The bar was filling up with smoke, and flames started to edge up the walls. He looked for the exits and ran to each, trying to get out. The doors were all barricaded shut. *Oh shit! What the hell is going on? Why can't I get out, and why did everyone leave me? Not even one damsel in distress to rescue.*

The flames were getting nearer and nearer. He was freaking out and screaming for someone to help him, but he'd been left all alone in this bar to burn alive.

Slowly the flames got closer. *Why am I not passing out from smoke inhalation? I can't burn alive. That's one of the very few ways I'd ever want to go. Why me? Why now? What did I do to deserve this? I sometimes go to church. Like six times per year.*

Soon, the flames latched onto him, and he caught on fire. He ran around the bar screaming and yelling obscenities as he felt the flames torching his every fiber. This lasted a few solid minutes, though it seemed like an eternity to him. He tried to run and fight every second of it and could feel the flames melting the bones in the tips of his toes through his body and up to his scalp. This continued until everything eventually went black.

Greyson woke up naked and hunched over in his cold metal chair. "Ah, Jesus! Not again! Come on! This is some bullshit!" he yelled.

He was then stood up, spun around, and placed in the bar again. He walked through the crowd and up to the bar to order a drink. All the women were staring at him with puzzled and disgusted looks on their faces. Confused, he looked at them with furrowed eyebrows. As he waded through the crowd to the bar, he got more disgusted faces from the hot women all around.

Confused, he tried to get to the bar faster. *They have those promotion mirrors with beer logos on them. I'll see what's going on and figure this out. Normally I get smiles or catch the eye of a chick. Not disgusted looks.*

He stepped up to the bar but didn't see in a mirror. He looked around for the restroom but didn't see one. He shrugged and ordered a drink anyway. He turned away from the bar to see what was happening, only to be greeted by more judgmental faces and stares. He quickly turned back in shame and put his head down on the bar. The bartender slid him his beer, and Greyson looked up to thank him.

He tipped his beer bottle back to take a long drink of the cool brew. He let out a sigh as the cold beer made its way through his esophagus. This helped soothe his anxiety but couldn't help prepare him for what would happen next.

He looked down at his beer bottle before taking another long gulp and was stunned to see his reflection in the glass. His features were completely charred. He immediately grabbed at the skin on his face. To his surprise, he couldn't feel anything.

He grabbed the bottle again and saw more disfigurement as the hotties around him whispered, trying to figure out what was wrong with him. Greyson set the bottle back down and turned to confront those who were mocking him. When he turned around, the bar was empty again. The doors were completely gone, and the room began filling with smoke again.

"Oh, for God's sake! This is really fucked up!" he screamed.

The sound of crackling fire began behind the bar near where he was standing. He downed his beer, thinking, *Well, I guess I'll go faster this time.*

No sooner than he thought that, the fire spread outward and all around him but not to him. He felt the full heat of the fire and anxiously awaited the feeling of being burned alive again. He stood there in a circle of flames while he waited and waited. He felt like his every molecule was melting away. Soon, the flames consumed him, and he spent longer burning, running around, and fighting it until everything went black.

CHAPTER EIGHT

K yle awakened in his cold metal chair again. He was naked and shaking, confused about why he was so cold. He was covered in near-freezing water as he sat in the chair. Unable to cross his arms to remotely bring any warmth to his core, he tried to speak but couldn't.

He instead thought, *What did I do to deserve this? I didn't make anyone freeze to death. I live in Florida. We get an occasional frost. Not like this tundra.*

The booming voice interrupted his thoughts: "You never made anyone freeze to death. But you made some freeze and wish for death!"

As soon as the voice was done speaking, a screen appeared. The reel started showing those he had violated curled up naked in cold showers as they cried. It showed one woman shaking in the shower as she cut her wrists.

Kyle started to feel razors slowly cutting his wrists like hers. The same spots, depth, and timing. He tried to reach across his body to grab his wrists to gain some comfort and control but couldn't. He had to sit and watch her cutting and shaking as he felt every bit of it. He started to cry and felt the tears freeze in his eyes.

With his eyes frozen open and unable to do anything else, he watched her cry and cut for hours. He was feeling remorseful at this point but still not fully grasping the whole concept of what was going on. This continued until it went black again.

He woke up in the chair again but with a full bladder. He tried to fight it again but gave in pretty quickly. He went through the cycle of painful urination and falling through the void. Then the painful urination and the spiders. Then the freezing and having to watch the woman cut herself. After many more rounds of suffering through his soul's deepest fears, he realized he may be in purgatory. He accepted that he had done wrong by many and must pay for his actions.

How long do I stay here? How long do I endure my own pain and suffering coupled with the pain and suffering that I caused others? What is next? Am I going straight to hell after this? Can I prove that I learned my lesson and will go right my wrongs? Is that even an option?

Ethel looked at Maddie and Machelle as Dan and Maddox looked on from her left and said, "See, some do have remorse. Can you feel how sorry he actually is? He is finally being reasonable and accepting his fate."

Maddie and Machelle asked, "How long is this going to be for him? He seems remorseful now."

Ethel replied, "Even some that are remorseful aren't quite to a level that we like. He is almost there, but he is at a point where he may think this is a bad dream if we send him back to the living. We must fully test his sorrows and ensure he has learned and will right his wrongs. We need to make sure he isn't just saying what we want to hear."

Dan asked, "What if he goes back and doesn't learn and acts the same way as he did before?"

Ethel replied, "We wait until he is asleep or driving by himself and then—sinkhole straight to hell. Screw that guy! Then he suffers forever. Oh, and Maddie and Machelle, never tell them how long. That gives them a timeline. We want them to think they are here for all eternity. That helps our ability to feel and judge their remorse. But whether they eventually get sent to hell or earn a trip back to the living—under probationary-style terms—our spots here fill up fast. It seems like a personal and intimate moment to them, which it is, but it's a fast-paced cycle for us. We're always busy."

Kyle continued through his cycles while the pain and extreme discomfort intensified. He truly did feel bad for his actions and figured this was his doing. He realized that he should accept it, not fight it. There was no way that any mortal soul could do this to him, let alone this be a prank.

He shrugged his shoulders and said to himself, *Screw it. This is my eternity. There is no seeing Mom again, and there is no going back to make things right. I deserve this and will pay whatever price.*

"What would you do should you be permitted to return to the living? How would you right your wrongs? You can't just sit here, feel sorry for your soul, and say you would make things right. How would you actually do it? When?" the booming voice commanded.

"I would turn myself in for my drinking and driving. Confess to date rape. For any date rape or assault that is too late to prosecute, I would go confess to the individual and offer to help pay for therapy. I'll quit drinking. I'll focus on helping people. I'll volunteer, doing whatever will help people. Even if it's filling sandbags in a hurricane. I'll be a better person—all the time," Kyle replied.

Ethel and the girls looked at each other. They turned to Maddox and Dan, seeking approval. Maddox said he could feel his remorse and believed him. Ethel went to get another judge to create a panel of five for the vote. Permitting one to return to the living required a majority of five votes. That is because of the dire consequences if they did not do as agreed upon or violated more rules.

The other judge came over and assessed Kyle's life, his time in purgatory, and his remorse levels. Ethel started the vote and moved that they permit him back to the living. Maddox agreed and suggested a strict follow-up on Kyle. Machelle agreed with sending him back to the living to right his wrongs, and she also agreed with Maddox. Maddie disagreed and believed he needed more time here, as she didn't want him harming anyone else if he wasn't as remorseful as he said he was. The additional judge believed he should go back to the living but also agreed with Maddie that he needed more time to prove himself there in purgatory than being placed back in the land of the living.

With the majority agreeing to send him back, they all decided that he needed more time to pay for his actions, and they would make it clear that there would be literal hell to pay should he not follow through. Until that discussion happened, he must continue on and on with his cycles.

While Kyle was in his area reliving the pain that he had caused everyone he had harmed, two new souls were waking up in their cold metal chairs. In the dark void, a dim light above them, screens appeared, and their lives started playing before them.

Dan stood there watching all of this unfold. He watched their confused faces wondering why they were naked and held down to a cold metal chair. He watched them freak out and cuss out their friends. "Okay, guys! You got me! Let me out now!" one shouted. Another threatened, "If you don't let me out soon, I'll whip your ass and beat your stupid faces in! Okay! Come get me out of here, assholes!"

Dan watched their faces change as the screen started playing through their lives. He studied their faces as the screens changed from happy times to their deepest darkest secrets and shameful actions. He watched their expressions of anger and horror as they got angry, wondering how someone could have such videos of them.

He quietly asked Maddox, "Why do they get so angry over the footage and how it was obtained? Why not feel guilty about their terrible actions?"

Maddox replied, "It's like in a court of law—they are pissed that they got caught, and there is evidence to punish them for their crimes. Otherwise, they would continue with their actions harming others. It's why they cry in court, begging for mercy. These are typically the ones who will fail to show any guilt while they are in here and are transitioned into hell. There is no way we can permit some like these two assclowns to go back to the living."

Dan just nodded and put his hand to his chin as he studied some more. He asked Maddox, "What's the ratio of those that feel true guilt and desire to do right versus these kinds of souls?"

Maddox looked at Ethel and replied, "Honestly, not many actually feel bad for their actions enough to make it out. We offer them the opportunity once they reach a certain level of remorse. It's all on them. We are more protectors for the living than helpers to those here in purgatory. They did the damage and need to figure it out on their own."

Dan, again, nodded and stayed focused on the two.

He was curious as to what their deepest fears would be and how they would be played out. One woke up on a couch in a pure black void and was confused. What appeared to be the tile of the floors in his living room appeared below him. He thought, *Phew! I didn't remember falling asleep on the couch, but whatever. I must have gotten wasted as fuck last night. Hope I don't have some skank in my bed.*

He noticed a couch cushion starting to move and tried to jump off the couch but couldn't. *What the fuck?* he screamed in his head. The cushion was moving beneath him, but he couldn't jump off. He kept squirming around but couldn't get off the couch. "Seriously, what the fuck is going on?" he tried to shout but found that no sound would come out.

More cushions started to move beneath him. He flailed about, trying to jump off the couch but encountered invisible barriers all around it. He tried to scream obscenities but couldn't. Then he tried to pass out, hoping he'd wake up and it would all be a bad dream. But he lay back again and noticed something that sent his panic into overdrive.

He looked to his left and saw an undeniable sight between the cushions and the backrest of the couch: the black and white scales of a rattlesnake tail moving. Then he saw the long rattle following the main body of the snake as it dipped back down under the seat cushions. He panicked but was now being held down by some unseen force. He watched as a wide triangular head appeared from under the cushion by his feet. The head of the snake was wider than the width of one of his palms.

The snake slowly slithered its way out of the cushion, bringing dirt with its scaly body. The snake slid up his foot and draped itself around his leg. As the rest of its body emerged from the cushions, it started to coil into a striking pose. Once the six-foot rattlesnake was fully revealed, it coiled into a rigid defense pose and aggressively shook its rattle to fully make its presence known and instill fear.

The man moved his hands to protect his privates, but they were stopped and held midair. In a confused panic, he tried again to maneuver his hands to his genitals and became violently angry after moments of struggling with his rigid muscles and joints.

He whimpered and closed his eyes, hoping to wake up in his bed or on his own couch, praying this was a bad nightmare. While his eyes were closed, he felt movement from under the cushion beneath his head. He tried to scream to wake up from this horrid dream, but nothing came out. He opened his eyes to see the big rattlesnake still coiled up between his legs in a striking position.

How is this not a bad dream? Why haven't I woken up yet? How is there a massive rattlesnake between my legs, and I can't move to protect myself? What else is in this couch? How did they get here? I swear on everything holy—I'll fuck up whoever thinks this is funny. Putting a venomous snake on my couch is not funny at all!

Just as he finished his last threat, the rattlesnake struck his hand. The inch-long fangs landed a strike on both the radial and ulnar nerves. He felt the pain of the fangs delivering the blows to his fixated hand. The rattler went back to the immediate defensive position, rattling away. He felt more movements in the cushions beneath him but couldn't move his head to see if it was another rattlesnake or something else.

As he watched the rattlesnake stay in a perfect pose, ready to strike again, he thought, *I don't think it injected any venom, just caused two minor flesh wounds. Worst-case scenario is a bad infection. That's an easy fix. Stupid-ass idiots—trying to harm me with a non-lethal snake. Fucking dumbasses will have to pay for their lame-ass attempt at a prank, though!*

No sooner than his last thought ended, he felt a sharp stabbing pain in his hand and severe swelling starting to take place. He couldn't move his hand. It stayed locked in the original position as it quickly started swelling.

The hand was swollen to the point of being glossy and discolored and oozed clear fluid at the fang injection sites. The swelling from the venom was too much for the hand to relieve, and the pain intensified. He was now feeling pain from the venom, the swelling, and the rapidly decaying tissue. The pain sensors in his arm were working overtime. He was in excruciating pain and was unable to scream.

Holy fuck! That has to be venom in my hand! An infection couldn't happen that fast! God! Please, someone help me!

He kept screaming in his head as the pain traveled up his arm. The swelling was so bad that his fingers were on the verge of bursting open like overcooked hotdogs on a barbeque. As he looked at his right hand and examined the full extent of the damage, he felt a sting in his left hand. *Ah, bitch!* he screamed in his head, knowing that his extreme pain was about to be twice as bad.

The rattlesnake went back into its striking position. The rattle was shaking but to a lesser extent. He looked at his left hand, feeling a smaller bit of pain, but he felt that could be masked by the untold amount of pain in his right arm. As the left hand started to swell and the pain intensified, the pain in his right arm traveled into his upper arm.

The pain in the right arm seemed to slow while the left hand grew intensely. Trying to see any silver lining, he thought the pain would stop around his biceps. He looked at the snake between his legs and moved his eyes from left to right. The snake was still in the same position but not going away. After what seemed like hours, the left arm pain and swelling caught up with the right side.

The pain picked up pace again and slowly etched its way to his core. *What kind of bullshit is this? Why me? Why can't I defend or protect myself? What kind of coward does some bullshit like this? This is seriously fucked up, man!*

A screen appeared above him, playing scenes from his dirty, dark secrets. The screen showed footage of him staying late at the office, zooming in from behind him as he calculated how much to transfer from the corporate accounts into his offshore account. It showed him falsifying documents that the finance department would look at. It showed him doing this for years, just enough to not raise suspicion and not get caught.

It showed him transferring most of the dividends from various clients' accounts into his offshore accounts. Again, just enough to show clients that they were gaining profits in their investments but with him skimming off their dividends beyond his contractual cut.

The video cut to him taking interns on small vacations while leaving his very pregnant wife at home. The video also showed him going to the doctor to get treated for an STD he got while on a work-related trip. It showed his wife finding the medications and him lying to her, telling her it was for a stomach infection.

The screen cut to static while the booming voice spoke, "That! That is *why you*! Your greedy little grabbers deserve to feel pain. You stole from hard-working people's retirement investments! *You* are the coward! You pranced around like you were a god when all the while, you were just a nasty thief! Stealing from your honest, hard-working clients! This is only the beginning!"

He couldn't formulate a response, and even when he thought he was ready to, the screen started playing again. It showed him in bed with an employee. She was a hard-working single mom trying to make it in the world and provide a life for her kid that she had only dreamed of as a child. It showed him telling her he loved her and would divorce his wife for her.

The scenes fast-forwarded through months of him continuing with this lie and leading her on. It showed her getting her two weeks' notice from the company and her looking at the stacks of bills. The scenes cut to her following him home and seeing his pregnant wife greeting him at the front door.

She was shown writing his wife a letter with evidence of their affair. It then showed her taking care of legal documents to make sure everything was lined up. Then it cut to an angle showing her writing another note while crying uncontrollably.

Just before the next scene happened, he felt the cushion under his head moving more. He felt something come up from the cushion and move around him. This appeared to be wider and heavier. He looked down and noticed the rattlesnake leaving the area between his legs. He tried to see if the screen would offer any reflection to see what was now around and on him.

The screen started and showed her placing a cup on the handwritten note now folded up on her nightstand. It showed her going downstairs and climbing on a ladder in front of the banister. She grabbed the hanging rope and placed it around her neck. As she did that, he felt the scales of a thick snake wrap around his neck.

She kicked the ladder out from under her feet, and the rope tightened around her neck, suffocating her. The boa constrictor tightened around his neck and slowly suffocated him as he watched her family find her and their torment. Then it showed him finding his lover's note to his wife in the mail. He watched the scenes cut back and forth while feeling the boa tighten more and more around his neck.

The scenes showed him burning the letter, then cut to her daughter being uprooted to her grandmother's house. The screen showed him going on and hurting others, including his own family, while her daughter endured many therapy sessions per week. It showed him being there when his daughter was born while her daughter was left to go to school and sporting events without her mom there to cheer her on and be a great friend and mentor.

The screen cut to black, and he blacked out too.

CHAPTER NINE

As he woke up to prepare for another battle of his version of purgatory, Kyle felt like his soul was exhausted, but he still had a fight in him. The fight wasn't one of anger or revenge but was driven by remorse and the desire to do right. Kyle wanted to prove he was worthy of returning to the living and staying with them. He wanted to right all of his wrongs and appreciate life for its true beauty.

Before the urinal and tile appeared, he said, "I know I fucked up. I really messed up in ways I would be ashamed to explain to my grandmother. I deserve this, but I would like to prove myself worthy of redemption—if it could ever be permitted. I would spend three thousand years here for a chance at three thousand hours back there. I'll spend every hour admitting my wrongdoing and make it right."

No booming voice responded to him. The tile floor and urinal didn't appear before him either. He was, instead, held into his chair, and the screen appeared before him. The video started playing his life again. He didn't think to complain about viewing this again because he was in no place to complain, nor would he ever be.

The video slowed down through the parts of his life where he had done the most harm. It played in real-time, as opposed to a fast-forwarded version like before. Throughout the scenes, he could feel every emotion and physical aspect of his victims. He felt the tears streaming down his face as he watched their tears fall. He felt his stomach churning, urges to vomit, and the cold sweats of a victim of his date rape as they awaited being called back for their first therapy appointment.

He felt the physical pain and the deep-rooted shame as another got a physical exam. He felt their pain of years of self-consciousness, weight gain, loss of self-confidence, and the emotional distress of finances from the therapy sessions and medications. He never realized how severe and lasting his consequences had been for them because of his selfish actions. He tried to divert his eyes for a break because the pain he felt in his soul was so strong. The screen just moved to the center of his focus.

He closed his eyes but couldn't escape it. *If I were granted three thousand hours out there, I must see this. I must endure the pain that I caused. Holy shit, this is a lot of pain, though. I just needed a quick break,* he thought.

"If I were somehow permitted to return, I would turn myself in right away. Accept a plea deal. Admit my actions so that I could be prosecuted for them and take any punishments. Those that I couldn't, I'd go admit it in person and deal with the consequences. I'd help pay for whatever I could to show my victims my most sincere apologies," he said out loud.

He was surprised when the screen turned to static, and the tile and urinal didn't appear before him. He was bewildered by it. He looked around into pure darkness, except for the faint light shining on him from an unknown distance. He looked around intensely as he held his breath, waiting to hear the sound of spider legs tapping on the walls around him. Nothing. Confused, he sat listening for any decibel of something sinister coming at him. A slight breath behind him? Nothing. The sound of footsteps or even a light breeze through the trees? Still nothing.

The light slowly dimmed. He turned his head trying to hear more, as he anticipated more torture. The light grew dimmer, giving way to the darkness of the void collapsing on Kyle. He slowly tilted his head as he squinted, hoping to capture a shadow while not allowing even a creaking joint in his neck to make a sound. Again, nothing.

It was nearly dark. Not dark enough to be pitch black but still light enough to cast a slight shadow of a human figure in a chair. He was anxious as he watched his shadow in the barely visible light. His heartbeat consumed all of the sounds his ears brought into his brain. His last effort to be prepared for anything coming at him was to stare at the shadow, hoping to catch a glimpse of something moving. Yet nothing. The light finally cut out, and all plunged into darkness.

Greyson woke up but not in a cold metal chair. He was lying on a hospital gurney in a surgery waiting area awaiting a hernia repair from an injury he'd suffered while playing football. It was his time to be wheeled back to the operating room. A medical team surrounded him, reassuring him that he would be okay. Lightly sedated, he was solely focused on the female nurse on the right side of the bed near the foot of the gurney, guiding it into the motion-censored double doors. The medication had him loopy and unable to speak, so he stared away.

The gurney wheels were locked and parked parallel to the operating table. He loved the tunes that the operating room staff had playing over a speaker while they finished the final steps to prepare for the repair. The staff helped him over to the table. They moved the monitors, IV tubing, and bag from the gurney to the operating room poles.

They started strapping him down with the restraints. The grounding pad was placed, and the OR nurse stopped everyone in the room to do a "time out." They identified the correct patient, procedure, and the surgery site, then noted any known allergies and adverse reactions.

The staff gave the anesthesiologist a nod. The anesthesiologist told Greyson that he would feel a burning in his arm in a moment but that it wouldn't last but a few seconds. Greyson soon felt the medication hit his arm and begin the trek to his brain. The medication hit him, and he tried to fight it as he quickly faded out. As his eyes rolled into the back of his head, he saw the anesthesiologist bringing the mask over his nose and mouth.

Greyson woke up anticipating a hot nurse hovering over him in the recovery room. Except that wasn't the case. As he started coming to, he heard the loud rhythmic beeping of the heart monitor. He saw the chin of the masked-up anesthesiologist as he conversed with the surgeons, nurses, and surgical technicians.

He realized he was still in surgery. He tried to scream or even squeak but completely failed. He tried to move his limbs but was held down by the paralytics and the restraints. He was in pure agony as he realized there was a laryngeal mask airway in his throat. His gag reflex began overtaking all of his thoughts, so much so that he forgot to try and make any movement to grab the attention of the anesthesiologist. Nothing would move except his eyes.

Oddly enough, his heart rate stayed at a normal seventy-two beats per minute with no indication of pain or his being awake. The whole operating room staff continued to discuss the past week's college football games, news, and the next week's game as they went about the surgery.

The monitors beeped in perfect rhythm. *What the fuck? Why is this guy not looking down at me? Isn't he supposed to be focused on the patient and not fucking sports? I'm so suing the shit out of this hospital when I get out of surgery! I'll own this stupid place and personally fire every single one of these assholes and then sue each of them for medical malpractice! This guy is the most incompetent turd on this planet!*

Greyson was stunned when he looked to the right of the anesthesiologist and saw a monitor screen go staticky. He tried to maneuver around again in hopes of really getting the attention of anyone at this point. Although he was fighting so hard in his mind to move anything in his body, nothing was working.

The screen started playing a scene of a dark night and a guy driving home from work. He was on the phone with his pregnant wife and their two other kids. He was reciting a bedtime story for his kids, just in case he didn't make it in time to tuck them into bed and kiss them goodnight. The father was focused on the road and his surroundings as he finished his story and told the kids he'd be home soon and would give them their goodnight kisses within thirty minutes.

He was driving along when a fast-moving vehicle with no headlights on came flying up on him and clipped his bumper. This caused him to fishtail and lose control until he rolled down the slight embankment. The speeding car continued with the music blaring.

The man's vehicle had an installed safety tracker, and the company noticed the abrupt speed change. They tried to communicate with him but couldn't get a response. They notified the local emergency medical services and state troopers. The screen showed the man being strapped to a spine board and airlifted to the nearest major trauma center.

The video showed the man receiving an MRI at the trauma center and the radiologist going over the results with his hysterical wife. A team of trauma surgeons and a counselor discussed with his wife that her husband appeared to be brain-dead. Then it cut to her reviewing the paperwork to end life support as tears fell on the papers.

The commandeered monitor-turned-screen showed Greyson driving fast without his headlights on while the music blared and the surroundings blurred past. He nearly fell asleep a few times but was just ten minutes from his house. He pulled into his garage at a jagged angle and crashed out in the recliner.

He woke up to his wife asking, "What happened to our sportster?"

He went out to take a look and said, "I don't know what happened. But don't worry, babe. I'll have Jose fix all the damages soon. I'll have him install the tinted windows we've been wanting while he's at it. Just clear a spot in the garage, and let's keep it in there until then."

The screen cut to an overview of Greyson lying on the operating table, and a split screen showed the brain-dead husband and father lying in his hospital bed as his wife looked at him, praying and begging for one more day with her husband and father of her kids. As one felt deep sadness for their completely altered life, one felt nothing but anger for no one paying attention to him. The latter screamed more obscenities and made more threats while the other wept for being unable to spend one more day with the love of her life. One heart was filled with hurt, the other with hate.

Greyson continued to scream obscenities and threats. *I'm definitely suing every fucking person in this operating room when I'm out of here. They're medical idiots, but somehow fucking spied on me too? So many violations! Done! Every single one of them! No mercy!*

Just then, the screen went back to the normal monitor screen. *Fucking good! About time they understand! It still won't lessen the blow I'll deliver!* he screamed internally again.

The anesthesiologist looked down at him and didn't say a word or even panic. *What the hell!? Not even an 'Oh shit! I just fucked up'? I'm going after this dickless moron first!* Greyson continued in his internal anger.

With a quick swivel in the chair, the anesthesiologist pressed some buttons and looked at the monitor quickly before looking back at the surgeons. The lack of sympathy pissed off Greyson even more, but before he could even think of another threat, his eyelids got heavy, and everything went black.

◇————◇

Greyson awakened fully clothed, standing in an amusement park roller-coaster line.

Huh. This is odd. I'm standing in line for a roller coaster, but I don't know any of these people. They are all a bunch of basics. But hey, at least the line is moving at a decent pace.

He kept scanning the crowd to see if he knew anyone in line. Or at least some hottie he could let cut the line so he could try to score.

All of his scanning while walking in the seemingly fast-paced line yielded no favorable results.

This sort of "freedom" freed his mind and consumed him to the point where he lost all situational awareness.

"Where does that line lead to?" Dan asked Maddox.

Maddox responded with glee, "Greyson has given up all situational awareness and is so consumed with his old ways that he fails to see what is going on."

"If you see, his two partners in crime are within a few feet from him," Ethel said in Dan's direction.

"We make their appearances generic to eliminate any recognition of one another. We do this for all," Ethel continued.

Maddox chimed back in, "They keep going into the dark tunnel without any concern."

Oh sweet! Finally about to board this bitch! I freaking love roller coasters! Greyson thought.

Unknown to Greyson, his buddy was sitting right next to him. *Not too bad! First row of this cart. Should be a great ride!*

Greyson looked around at the flickering lights in the dark tunnel as he boarded.

"So glad to be doing something fun again. I felt like I was in this terrible nightmare," he said aloud.

He turned to see if his front-row partner heard him.

His buddy, still unknown to him, looked around mindlessly with a basic facial expression.

"Are you okay?" Greyson asked him.

He said something, but it was so garbled that Greyson couldn't comprehend it.

Great! I'm sitting next to a Mumble McGee!

As soon as he finished his thought, he felt the brakes on the track release, and they started a slow roll.

The speed started picking up, and the passengers felt themselves being strapped down tighter into their seats.

The speed was ramping up more and more.

Holy shit! This has to be the fastest roller coaster in the world! he thought as his eyes became dry and his hair flew parallel with the tracks.

Oh! Dear God! What the hell is that smell? I never knew of a roller coaster getting anywhere around sulfur. Ugh!

He tried to look around but couldn't. Between the cart's straps and the coaster's speed, he was completely pinned back in his seat.

What the hell? Why is it getting so hot?

It was getting so hot that he felt the plastic melting around his flesh and clothes. The smell of the sulfur and the heat were making the metal too hot for him to grip. He sank into the hard plastic of the seat as he screamed.

The cart started to slow down, but everything kept getting hotter. He and his companions were melted into their seats.

As the cart neared a stop, they all blacked out.

CHAPTER TEN

In a cool, muddy, and grassy swamp, Kyle awakened. The lower half of his body was submerged in the insect-infested water, his upper body easing out of the water but still in the tall grass. The sounds of crickets chirping in the night sky and frogs hunting easily targeted insects surrounded him. He lay there silently, breathing for a few moments as he tried to assess everything.

After gathering information about his surroundings, he tried to crawl but failed. The pain he felt was so intense that it took his breath away. He winced in pain and tried again with more strength. He barely gained any traction as he slipped and caused more pain.

He didn't get frustrated, though. Instead, he used his unbroken left arm to push himself up enough to use his hip and torso to rotate himself on his back. He flopped in the cool muddy clay of the swamp. He was grateful to be looking up at a clear night sky, the glow of city lights in the distance. He lay there on his back and, although cold, was happy to be staring at countless stars. The cold creeping in caused him more pain, but he had no complaints.

He shimmied his way up the bank and fully out of the water and insect-ridden marsh. He pushed backward until he reached a dry spot where he could use his left arm to pick himself up enough to get a leg far enough back to stand up. That motion caused a lot of pain, but he needed to get to a doctor for X-rays to see the full extent of the damage.

He started hobbling toward the road, where he saw an occasional passing vehicle. He figured that would take him to a town. As he walked and focused on the direction of town, he took many glances up at the beautiful clear sky in a deep appreciation for the universe's beauty. He had a renewed appreciation for the beauty of life, and although he was in immense pain, he was still taking in the beautiful night sky.

A car slowed down behind him about two miles into his painful walk. He moved over further off the road to wait for the car to pass, but it slowed down even more. He used his left arm in an attempt to wave them past. The car stopped behind him. He fully turned and squinted into the headlights in the dark of night. The headlights were directly on him, and he again waved the vehicle to pass but to no avail.

"Say, son. What are you doing out here all by yourself? You okay?" a deep Southern voice asked.

"I'm by myself. Just trying to get to that town over there," Kyle said as he winced in pain while trying to point with his broken right arm and collarbone.

"You okay there, son? You appear to be in some pain," the voice questioned.

"Do you know what town that is and if they have an emergency room? I'm pretty banged up."

"Yeah, I'd say so! That town has a little urgent care but not for injuries or ailments like you have, son. I'm a deputy sheriff and can take you or call you an ambulance. Either way, let's get ya taken care of."

Kyle stood there for a moment in what appeared to be hesitation, but it was more of a deep-rooted thought.

"Son? You okay?"

"Uh, yeah. Sheriff, my name is Kyle, and I need to turn myself in. I was involved in an accident and fled the scene," Kyle confessed.

The deputy approached him with his hand on his taser in a defensive manner. As the sheriff got closer, he could see that Kyle was the man they had been searching for over the past few hours. The sheriff radioed in his location and requested an ambulance.

Kyle sat on the ground and told the sheriff, "Sir, I don't have any ill intent for you or anyone else. I know I'm a wanted man that fled the scene of an accident, and you have to be ready to defend yourself, but I'll lay here and cooperate. I'm in so much pain and filled with so much guilt."

The surprised sheriff stood there and talked with the broken-down man. They didn't discuss any of the things Kyle promised to confess later. Kyle was mostly inquisitive about jail and what to expect. The two talked man-to-man, human-to-human. This was eye-opening to both. A wanted man that avoided capture on multiple accounts and a sheriff that had encountered the worst of the worst.

The ambulance arrived shortly after the deputy's backup, and the desolate road was soon awash in flashing lights. Kyle was loaded into the back of the ambulance with a handcuff on his left wrist, shackling him to the bed rail of the gurney. The doors shut, and the long ride to the nearest hospital began.

The paramedic did a full assessment, radioed in a report to the waiting emergency room doctor, and started an IV. Kyle refused the IV at first by saying, "I don't want any pain medicine unless it's absolutely necessary. I deserve this pain."

The paramedic was bewildered by Kyle's initial response and assured Kyle he wouldn't unless necessary. He told him it was to gain access to the vein to push any meds that could be needed, either in the ambulance or at the hospital. Kyle nodded and continued to feel the extreme pain with every bump in the road.

The emergency room doctor and her team met the ambulance and began their initial intake and exam. They ordered X-rays, a CT scan, an MRI, and various labs. The doctor could see fractures of the right ulna, humerus, clavicle, and several ribs. He notified the on-call orthopedic surgeon while Kyle was sent to get the images done. He came back with his hospital escort and the deputy assigned to the prisoner transport.

"Sheriff, can I use my one phone call?" Kyle asked the deputy assigned to him.

"We can allow that. Make it quick. I'll notify the jail that you've already used your one call," the deputy responded, handing him the hospital room phone.

Kyle dialed seven digits and awaited an answer.

"Mom? Yeah, I'm fine. I'm at the county's general hospital," he said before his mom interrupted him, exclaiming her concern so loudly that he had to hold the receiver farther away from his ear.

"Yes, Mom. I'm well enough to talk. Can you call Jerry and tell him I have to confess to some things? Yes, confess. I messed up really bad, Mom—" he tried to squeeze in more before she interrupted him again, her emotions turning to anger.

"You do know your rights, right?" the deputy whispered loudly to Kyle. "You were read them before I got here, correct? Because anything you are about to say can and will be used against you in a court of law."

Kyle put the phone down and said, "Yes, sir. I was read my rights, and I'm aware. Thank you, sir."

Kyle held the phone down a moment to let his mother's emotions subside, and he let some of the pain pass from holding the phone to his ear.

He continued, "Mom, please bring Jerry down to the hospital. I'll probably be going back into surgery at some point. Love you, Mom."

Kyle thanked the deputy and awaited his hysterical mother's arrival. "I'm honestly more afraid of my mom than of surgery or jail. She is terrifying. I mean, you heard her going off on me on the phone," Kyle said to the deputy.

The deputy laughed because he had seen angry, emotional mothers plenty of times during his time as a deputy in the jails. He planned on leaving the lawyer and the mother in the room with the prisoner while he guarded from outside the room in hopes of hearing what went down.

"Where is my son? Kyle Farmer! He called about twenty minutes ago! Where is he?" Kyle's mom yelled at the nurse at the nursing station.

Kyle, and the whole first floor of the hospital, heard.

In a sarcastic tone, with a cheeky grin, the deputy said, "Hey, I think your mother is here."

Kyle felt his gut start churning and regretted turning down the pain medicine to relax him for what was heading his way next.

An ER nurse walked Mrs. Farmer to the door with their family lawyer in tow. The two entered, and she hugged Kyle with a massive momma-bear hug. He winced but dared not complain about the pain the hug caused. His mom pulled back and swung her purse angrily at her son as she noticed the left handcuffed to the raised railing. She knew his right side was injured, but she wasn't exempting herself from delivering some angry blows to his unprotected left side.

The sheriff smiled as he watched through the small door window and then turned away to allow the prisoner to speak to his attorney in privacy.

Kyle braced himself for a long-winded confession to his lawyer and mother. As he explained his wrongdoings, his lawyer recorded and took notes. His mom sat in the corner chair sobbing uncontrollably with mixed emotions. He lay there sobbing as he hurt for his victims and how much he had hurt his mother's heart.

The knock on the door ended the confession, and the orthopedic surgeon entered to discuss the imaging results and treatment plans. "Mr. Farmer, you have extensive damage to your right arm and clavicle. Seeing as these are open fractures, we need to go in and fix them tonight. We have an operating room that will be ready soon. We really can't send you to the jail for processing and to be incarcerated without getting this done. We will get the consent done, and the other doctor will come in and go over the risks and possible complications, not that we anticipate any, but just so you are aware of the risks. I'll see you in the OR in a bit."

"Thank you, sir," Kyle responded, his head hung low.

After some waiting, a slew of medical staff came in and out of the ER holding area to prepare him for surgery. He filled out consent forms, administration papers, admission paperwork, insurance information, his medical history, family medical history, and any other legal form. His mom sat in the corner, watching her son with a new mindset. Was she staring at her son or a monster? Or was he both?

She got up and left to go into the waiting room, and the lawyer, Jerry, soon followed when the room became crowded with medical staff. He went to comfort and reassure her that people can be truly remorseful and that Kyle's confession and turning himself in was a huge step in that direction.

Kyle was wheeled into the operating room, and the anesthesiologist finally pushed some medication to relax him, as he noticed Kyle was starting to shake with anxiety. The medical team transferred Kyle to the operating table. He was relieved to be getting fixed so he could work on righting his wrongs.

The staff stopped all movement in the operating room and did a time out. As the OR managed the procedure, Kyle looked around the operating room at the staff, the instruments, and the monitors. He tried to focus on the OR nurse's commanding voice, but something caught his eye while he pondered the operating room scene.

A message scrolled across the fluoroscopy machine. *You have one hundred and twenty-five days, or three thousand hours, to right your wrongs! You are commended on your confession! Keep after it! Bye for now!*

Kyle blinked several times to see if he had seen that right, but the screen went back to black while the team finished their prep. Kyle was a bit freaked out and didn't want to be put under. Just then, the anesthesiologist started pushing the syringe full of propofol. The clear IV tubing full of saline soon turned white with the strong mixture.

"Your arm could feel a bit of a burning sensation, and you may feel a bit fuzzy, but it will be short-lived. Just relax and breathe the oxygen through the mask while the medication works," the anesthesiologist said.

Kyle felt the slow, slight burning in his arm and felt it go from his hand up to his shoulder. Soon after, he felt the operating room surroundings collapsing as everything faded into darkness.

Before he fully went out, he heard a loud ringing in his ears and a booming voice said, "ONE HUNDRED AND TWENTY-FIVE DAYS!"

Startled, he tried to fight it, but the propofol was too powerful to even make him wince before he was consumed by darkness again.

<hr />

"Holy fuck, that was some messed up shit! That one dude, what was his name? Greyson? That guy was a psychopath that was hell-bent on blaming others for his disgusting actions," Machelle said as she and Maddie grabbed their belongings in the break room at Used Books Plus.

In a wide-eyed stare, Maddie chimed in, "Phew, those were some dark souls! I'm glad they aren't back up here anymore."

"Unfortunately, there are still dark souls here among the living. It's on us to help protect good people from them. Still, it's weird to think how Ethel sent those three straight to hell. I guess there was no way they were ever going to feel any remorse. Oh well. What are you thinking for some food?" Machelle replied as she gently grabbed Maddie's shoulder while she walked by to bring her out of her trance.

"I don't know, really. I'm kind of in the mood for a toasted sandwich. What about you?" Maddie cheerfully said as she turned and headed to the front door.

"Sounds good to me. God, it feels like we've been gone forever, but it has only been a few hours. I almost said, 'Shit, your mom must be uber worried about you and looking everywhere,' but then I looked at the clock and date. I'm still hungry as can be, though," Machelle said with a grin.

The two girls checked their phones to see what they had missed out on while they were absent from the mortal world. Nothing but negative stuff in the news and some texts from classmates or family. They drove off to get some sandwiches but didn't want to sit in the restaurant and eat while talking. They wanted to eat and debrief about their first encounters in purgatory and being on the panel.

Prior to going into the sandwich shop, they each turned on their karma display to get readings on the workers. They studied the karma levels of the employees and were a little cautious about their sandwiches when they got back to the car because the two making them had fairly low scores. Maddie and Machelle didn't know if it was for improper food service or something else, but they gave their food an extra look-see when they were in the parking lot.

"Let's pull up some local news articles and see what we can see on the karma scales. Maybe we'll see some crazy shit," Maddie said as she indulged in her meatball sub with a sip of her favorite locally made soda.

"Speaking of crazy!" Machelle said as she set her sandwich back down. "That Kyle! He was feeling his guilt. It was very refreshing to see that after processing all those others."

"I wonder what the ratio is of those who return to those that stay there or get sent to hell. I don't even know if that scale is worth looking at. That sounds like a question for Ethel later," Maddie said as she prepared for another bite.

The girls bantered back and forth throughout their meal before heading back to Maddie's house.

"Hey, have you heard from AJ lately?" Machelle asked Maddie.

"You know me, I just reach out and contact everyone."

"Oh, I know. But has she reached out to you?" Machelle continued.

"No. I haven't heard anything." Maddie crumpled her sandwich wrapper.

Machelle eagerly picked up her phone and scrolled to AJ's contact information before punching the *call* button.

"Hello?" AJ's voice sounded excited.

"Hey, girl! I got Maddie here, and you're on speaker. What's up?"

"I am uploading all of my footage from my trip. How are y'all doing?" AJ chattered.

"Oh, nice. You'll have to tell us all about it soon," Maddie chimed in.

"It's loading up now," AJ mumbled, her mouth full of something crunchy.

"How was your trip back? When do you start classes? Are you going into freshman year single, or is there someone special?" Machelle said as she sipped her drink.

"Yeah. Uneventful trip back home, and yeah, going into my first semester of college solo. But at least I will stay focused and not be—"

"Not be what?" Machelle asked.

Machelle and Maddie looked at each other as the silence stretched out for a few moments.

"Not be what?" Maddie asked this time.

AJ still didn't respond.

In sync, they said, "Not be *what*? AJ, talk to us!"

"Uh, I gotta... I gotta go," AJ said, her voice sounding strange.

"No! Don't go! Talk to us," Maddie pleaded.

"Ma! You gotta see this!" AJ said as the line clicked and went silent.

Mel was eagerly awaiting her daughter's return so she could hear about her and Machelle's time together. She was on the front porch glider when the two girls pulled up and got out. Mel noticed the light bag from Sammy's Slammys.

"Let me guess, Maddie had the meatball sub and the local cherry cola?" Mel chuckled as she turned to open the door. "And what did you have, Ms. Machelle?" she pressed.

"I had the Danwich. It was pretty good but can be messy. Definitely not a sandwich for driving," Machelle said.

"The Danwich?" Mel questioned as she grabbed her daughter a fresh local cherry cola.

"Yeah, it's two peanut butter and jelly sandwiches in one but with only three pieces of bread. That way, you get more peanut butter. The middle piece has peanut butter on both sides. Because, you know, otherwise, the bread absorbs the jelly. That's just gross. You gotta make a PB&J the right way, not the weak way."

"Hmm... you know... I'll have to try that sometime soon."

"Well, we've had a long day, and I should get going. Maddie, see you tomorrow?"

"Yeah, it won't be until later in the day, though," Maddie replied. "I'm exhausted and want to decompress, if you know what I mean."

"Absolutely. No rush. I completely understand," Machelle said as she waved to Mel and headed out.

"A lot of customers today?" Mel vaguely asked

"Yeah. Very unfortunate, had many customers today," Maddie grumbled as she sipped her soda and stared out the big front window.

"Yeah, unfortunately there are a lot of customers sometimes, but hopefully you did your best and did right by them all," Mel continued.

Maddie cocked her head, a little confused by what her mother meant. She excused herself to go upstairs and call it a day.

What does she mean? Why was she being so vague? This is all so confusing. We've never talked about how many customers come to the store. Today is the first day she's ever even mentioned it. Maybe I'm making a big deal over nothing. I need some sleep.

Maddie closed her eyes to escape it all and hoped to wake up the next day with renewed energy and hope for the world around her.

"Sir, how are you feeling?" asked the post-anesthesia care unit, or PACU, nurse.

Kyle jolted awake in the hospital bed, held down by the pain from the upper portion of his chest on the right side to his wrist. The handcuffs still restrained his other wrist.

"No need to jump out of your bed just yet. You should be in no rush to get out of here. Lay there and relax while the anesthesia wears off. How are you doing regarding your pain?" The PACU nurse spoke as she looked at the monitors and her computer.

"It hurts, ma'am. If I could get something for the pain, I would be very appreciative," Kyle asked the nurse.

"Let me see what the doctor has ordered for breakthrough pain medicine, and I'll get right back to you," she responded.

Kyle lay there with his eyes closed, dozing in and out of consciousness.

"Sir, I'm going to administer two milligrams of Dilaudid through the IV," the nurse announced. She then let him know she was right there and what she was going to do for him to help prevent him from being startled.

With his eyes still closed and in a slightly less groggy voice, he replied, "Thank you, ma'am. You nurses are underappreciated, and I just want to say thank you. I know it might not mean much because I'm handcuffed to the bed here, but seriously, thank you."

He felt the medication take over and mix with the anesthesia that was slowly wearing off. He was awakened again by the feeling of the bed moving and the staff telling the deputy where they were going.

As the bed was being wheeled down the hallway to the same-day surgery ward, Kyle was now wide awake as he heard the deputy's gear clanking with every step and the bed wheels going over every bump along the way. The deputy looked down at his prisoner and smiled as they neared the ward.

Kyle could hear a familiar voice in the room as he talked with the family lawyer and an unfamiliar voice. Still groggy, he thought it must be one of Jerry's paralegals.

The bed was positioned and locked. The deputy grabbed a chair and sat right outside the room to let his prisoner discuss more with his attorney.

"Kyle, how are you feeling?" Jerry asked.

"I'm doing all right. No reason to complain. I did this to myself. More people are hurting because of me. So, who am I to complain?" Kyle responded after he saw the disappointed look on his mother's face.

"This is the prosecutor who is working your case. Well, apparently other cases—after what you told me."

The prosecutor spoke next. "You are being charged with drunk driving, fleeing the scene of an accident, and possession of narcotics. You have already been read your rights, and your attorney told me that you are very adamant about signing a plea deal to those. Is that correct?"

With a glance at his mother, he turned his head back and bowed it as he answered, "Yes, sir. That is correct, and I would like to confess to some other things too. I want to plead guilty on all counts and work with you on punishments. If at all permissible, I'd be grateful if I could plead out, post bail, and recover at home until I'm healed enough to serve my time. I'll surrender my passport, wear one of the fancy ankle monitors, and do anything you ask. I messed up big time. I'll volunteer for therapy and Alcoholics Anonymous. Whatever the court asks of me."

Jerry asked for a few moments alone with his client before Kyle kept talking in his drugged-up state. The prosecutor obliged and excused himself to wait outside. He closed the door behind him.

"Kyle, I did some research the past few hours, and there are some cases that you'll be prosecuted for, but some fall outside the statute of limitations. However, that may not stop someone from coming forward with a civil suit. Are you sure you want to press forward? I highly recommend you go get processed for what you are currently being charged with. Then post bail and go home to be of a fresh mindset. Then we can reapproach. Does that sound fair?" his attorney advised him.

"Yes, sir. I need to kick the meds from my system, and with a clear mind, it will help give me the assurance I need. Plus, I know I shouldn't be signing any legal documents under these conditions anyway," Kyle wisely responded.

The attorney nodded and went to go walk and talk with the prosecutor while his client began to prepare for his exit from the hospital and into the processing of the criminal justice system.

CHAPTER ELEVEN

Dan and Maddox enjoyed a mixed drink in Maddox's limo as they cruised through the world-famous Strip at night. Dan took a few big drinks from his tall glass as he tried to process everything he had just witnessed. He looked at all the lights and tall buildings as the limo slowed to a stop at another red light.

"How do you do it?" he asked Maddox as he stared at the many blinking lights.

"I just do it. It's a task that needs to be done," Maddox vaguely responded between sips.

Dan continued with more questions, "Like, how do you process it? You see the worst souls that have walked this earth. How does one do that and come back smiling?"

"I do it to help protect the other seven billion people on the planet, and I smile knowing that I do it for those who deserve better," Maddox replied as he looked at Dan, who stared straight ahead in complete shock.

"How do you know who is good and who is bad? How can you look at someone and tell? We can't trust the justice system. How can you send someone to purgatory for serving a life sentence for having weed on them while a corrupt politician gets six months for embezzlement, voter fraud, cheating, scandals, and God knows what else? How do you guys do it?"

"Here, let me show you something," Maddox said to Dan as he waved his hand and brought up a transparent screen against the limo window. He continued, "You see the little gauges that look like gas tanks next to everyone walking down the street? That's their individual karma level. Do you see how each person's is different— how some fill up and some drop? You can see them changing even as we sit at this long red light."

Dan was completely sober now and totally intrigued. He nodded, waiting for Maddox to continue.

Maddox urged him to take a selfie to show Dan his karma level. This piqued Dan's interest. He was past the purgatory scene and fully focused on the present moment.

"See, your level is about eighty-six percent. Nobody is ever fully at a hundred. So, you probably told someone to kiss your ass, passed judgment, or had road rage or something recently. Trust me, eighty-six is good," Maddox said as he deleted the image.

"Why are you telling me all of this? Why did you take me into purgatory?" Dan questioned Maddox.

"You saw something that you weren't supposed to. A version of me in your geographical region messed up and allowed a witness. You weren't supposed to see a car with three people disappear. Someone failed. That certain someone has been, um, let go," Maddox answered.

"What do you mean 'let go'? Were they one of the ones I saw in purgatory?" Dan nervously asked.

"Ha!" Maddox laughed. "No, they are no longer part of MaCoven. When someone messes up or fails in any way that could compromise our existence, their minds are completely cleared of everything to do with us, and they go about their lives like nothing happened. We also do the same for those that want to leave MaCoven or retire. Look, the reason I'm telling you all of this is because you've already seen a car disappear and what we do," Maddox said as he wiped his hand in the opposite direction, and the transparent screen disappeared.

Maddox sat there in the moving limo and watched Dan take a few more drinks. He could see Dan's wheels turning with many confused blinks and squints of his eyes. Dan pressed the button to open the sunroof and stood up to breathe some fresh air. It was late August summer-night hot air, but at least it was fresh.

Dan dipped back down into the limo and stirred a newly made strong drink before standing up again in the sunroof to fully take in all the scenes of the heart of the Strip. Maddox made another drink and joined Dan. He didn't say anything else while he and Dan enjoyed their drinks and the views.

After a few moments of thinking, Dan asked, "Why me? I know I already asked that but why? You could have just wiped my mind clean too, and I would have thought it was a crazy dream or something."

In a deadpan tone, Maddox said, "Well, we now seem to find ourselves with an opening."

With a stunned smile, Dan chuckled. "Yeah, I get that!"

Maddox quickly interjected before Dan could say more, "You have good karma levels, and we thought with what you witnessed coupled with your levels, you would potentially be a good fit."

"I don't know. I'd have to seriously think about it. That was some seriously messed up shit! I'm sure that was just a glimpse, too," Dan skeptically replied.

"It was just a preview of what takes place and what we do. It's crazy and takes a special individual to do it, but a few of us believe that you would be good at it. You just go about your days as you normally would—working, vacationing, and whatnot, but you would have a moral code to do right by people. You would be a silent guardian, if you will," Maddox explained.

Dan took another swig from his strongly mixed drink and looked out at everyone as they went about their hot summer night in Sin City. He took a few more drinks and was about to speak.

Before Dan could formulate a response, Maddox sharply said, "No rush on a decision. Take your time and think it over. I'll check back in after a while, though. Let's get you back to your room so you can rest up and head back."

The limo pulled up to the front entrance of the hotel and casino.

The two shook hands and went about their night. Dan didn't head to bed, though. He stayed on the casino floor and had a few more drinks while playing some games at the tables.

The next day, Dan checked out of the hotel a bit later than he had planned but was surprised when he went to the rideshare exit of the hotel and casino. He saw Maddox's limo driver with a sign and the limo ready for Dan to take to the airport.

Throughout the journey through the airports, and as he settled into his flight, Dan kept thinking about it all. He kept pondering how many evil souls there must be to have a whole secret group out there protecting the innocent and unsuspecting. He jotted down some questions for Maddox when they could have a lengthy discussion again.

Kyle awaited his sheriff's escort to the local courthouse for his initial hearing before the magistrate. Jerry said he'd meet them at the courthouse. He advised Kyle not to talk much because it could damage his plea deal and any ability to fully recover at home and affect the length of jail time he'd have to serve.

Kyle and Jerry stood tall before the magistrate at the initial hearing. Kyle kept his head hung low and respectfully answered the magistrate when directly addressed.

"I'll grant you bail under the circumstance that you heal at home, you remain under house arrest, and anytime you go to or from the hospital, you'll have a sheriff's deputy with you at all times. I have your passport—thank you for surrendering that in advance and taking the initiative. Should you break any of the terms, your bail will be revoked, and you'll be placed in custody. When your surgeon gives you the clearance, you are to return to the county jail to be processed and await your sentencing. Am I clear?" the magistrate said.

"Yes, sir. Very clear," Kyle said in a shameful tone.

The deputy escorted Kyle to his house and activated his new

ankle monitor. The deputy put it on his ankle nice and snug. The deputy said he would be back for his follow-up appointment but would be watching his every move. Kyle seemed a bit creeped out by that but figured he would just be monitoring the GPS tracker in the ankle bracelet.

A few short weeks had passed since Kyle's incident and his surgery. He was feeling better and less in pain, except when a storm was near, and he could feel the aching in his bones from the breaks and the surgical hardware. When he wasn't working out in the in-home gym, he spent a lot of time doing some writing. He felt really bad about all the wrongs he had committed and was afraid of messing up and ruining his second chance.

The afternoon of his follow-up, he had the garage door open and was between bicep curl sets and just sat there and watched the life around him. He felt a new appreciation for the birds playfully fighting in the trees. He was grateful to be able to see the different shades of greens of the leaves, the bushes, and the grass. He took notice of the beautiful light-blue sky with amazing white puffy clouds perfectly scattered about the vast blue expanse. He appreciated the sounds of the wind through the trees.

He knew that in a matter of hours, he would be staring at concrete walls that would encapsulate him for an unknown amount of time. For the first time in his life, he quit his workout and just appreciated the little, yet finer, things that surrounded him. He had a newfound appreciation for owning his wrongdoings, accepting punishments, and life itself.

The deputy pulled up and went to deactivate the ankle bracelet and then put Kyle in handcuffs. On the drive to the clinic, Kyle asked the deputy to have the windows down or cracked, so he could appreciate the sounds of the wind and feel the fresh air. The deputy obliged and rolled the windows down about halfway as they cruised over to the hospital.

"Welp, good news, Mr. Farmer. Your X-rays indicate that your bones are healing up nicely with the assistance of the surgical hardware. Your incisions are all healed up as well. You have a clean bill of health. Deputy, he is all yours," the orthopedic surgeon told Kyle.

The deputy said, "All right now, son. Let's get going to the county jail to get you all processed."

Without hesitation, Kyle stood up and turned, facing the window while the deputy placed the cuffs on him again and grabbed him by the lower end of the forearm, near the wrist.

Throughout the short ride to the county jail, Kyle kept savoring the fresh air and looking at the beautiful scenery. He even appreciated the partially cloudy sky being reflected off a still lake just minutes from the facility. Kyle hoped he could have a window that looked out on the beauty of the life surrounding him. He even pondered about asking to be sent to a medium-security prison facility so he could work outside. He hoped to be helping rescue animals, trimming palm trees, or even picking up trash.

After the deputy dropped Kyle off to begin his processing, he returned to his cruiser, eager to finish his shift paperwork and start the next day with something fresh. The deputy checked to ensure he had everything all set, including the ankle bracelet to return to the station. He pulled out his cell phone before he pulled up his laptop to finish the paperwork.

Kyle Farmer is at the county jail now. He is processed and awaiting his sentencing. He should be in for a good while. He seems remorseful enough, and he opened up about sending letters before going to his clearance appointment today. On to the next. Have a good rest of your day, Ethel.

"I really wish we had some timeline on our probation time," Maddie said to Machelle as they entered Used Books Plus.

"I know. Me too. But I'm sure they have this system for a reason. They are investing so much time and trust in us. I'm sure there is so much to it all, and we have barely scratched the surface," Machelle said in agreement with Maddie.

"I mean, I get the whole protecting the group and all, but that whole purgatory stuff was super intense," Maddie continued.

"I hear ya, but again, I think it's all for a good reason, and they need to ensure we do right without biased decisions. If you think about it, so many souls are in our hands. Both here and in purgatory. They need us to see all the aspects and to keep the secret hidden. Greater good for the greater number kind of thing," Machelle explained to comfort her friend and cohort.

"I know, I know. Oh, did I tell you what my mom asked about the other day? It really freaked me out," Maddie excitably stated.

"No. You didn't tell me. Was this right when we got back, and I dropped you off?"

"Yeah. She never asks about the bookstore or customers. Well, other than a quick, 'how was your day?'" she said as they grabbed a box of books and brought them to the shelves to be sorted and filed. "Well, she asked if we had a lot of customers and if we did right by them. So, freaking strange. It was on the day of our first purgatory trip."

Puzzled, Machelle responded, "That is odd. What did you say?"

"I looked at her with a weird look and said, 'Yeah, we had a lot of customers today.' And that's when she said she hoped I did my best and did right by every customer," Maddie vented in confusion.

"Yeah, that definitely sounds freaking weird as shit. And, especially on that day."

The two continued to do inventory while chatting about purgatory again. They carried on for a few hours.

"I'd say it's about lunchtime. Not sure if you can hear my stomach growling," Machelle exclaimed.

"Absolutely, it *is* that time! And yes, your stomach is just as chatty as you," Maddie said in a playful, sarcastic manner.

Machelle chuckled a bit and then responded, "What would you say to walking over to the nearest outlet of shops? They have a decent food court. I need some fresh air."

"Yeah. That sounds good. And same."

The two finished their task and hastily locked up to stop their stomachs from chatting back and forth. As they walked and talked, they heard something that scared them.

"Oh my god! Do you hear that? That sounds so terrible! Like a wounded animal!" Maddie yelled as she took off running.

"I do! And yes, it does!" Machelle was nearly yelling as she started a sprint behind Maddie.

To their complete disgust, they turned the corner down a narrow street. They ran to a small yard surrounded by a chain-link fence where they found a man cheering on as the two dogs fought in a modified cage.

"Hey!" Maddie screamed.

"*Hey!*" she screamed again as she sprinted closer.

"HEY! STOP!" the two screamed together.

The man grabbed one of the dogs and put him in a separate cage. The dogs whimpered in pain as they licked their wounds while getting a few drinks of water.

The man stormed over to the fence. "What the hell are you two doing? Sniffing your noses around places they ain't supposed to be sniffing!" he growled menacingly.

"Are you intentionally harming those dogs?" Machelle asked in a high-pitched and emotional tone.

"And if I was, it's none of your damn business. Now you best be getting before I release them on you two," he said as he turned his back to them and began to walk away. "Stupid-ass bitches. Poking your noses around here."

With a snap of Maddie's finger, he disappeared.

Machelle looked surprised at how fast Maddie had responded but was equally proud of her for acting so decisively.

"Well, let's call Ethel really quick. We have to let her know and find out how to get the dogs the help they need without raising concerns over where the owner is," Machelle said as Maddie stared at the poor dogs.

"Hey, Ethel. We have to let you know that we just sent a man straight to purgatory. He was training dogs to fight or something. We are worried about what to do to get the dogs the help they need," Machelle said through the phone.

Ethel responded, "Get some food and get back to the store. I'll make a call as a concerned neighbor and say that he drove away with a known drug dealer, and the humane society will pick up the dogs."

The girls barely had an appetite but knew they needed something in their stomachs because it was looking to be a while before they would get a chance to eat again.

They arrived back at the store and ate fast. They didn't talk much but were both excited to see this one through. It was personal, and they felt so bad for those dogs. The more they thought about it, the angrier they got.

Maddie thought, *How can someone purposely breed animals with such cruel intentions? And for what? Entertainment? Money? Both? How could someone do such a thing? To bring intentional harm to an animal for their own benefit. Knowing damn fucking well that those poor dogs will suffer in pain and die so young!*

Maddie got her trash and angrily threw it away. She walked to the door, locked it, and dimmed the lights. She walked back, grabbed Machelle's trash, and threw it away too.

"Let's fucking go!" she said with a fiery tone.

The two disappeared.

Dan decompressed the whole flight from Las Vegas to San Diego. He'd had a strong drink at the Vegas airport, a double, to be exact. He couldn't help but think of everything he had witnessed. He kept going over everything in his mind while he stared out at the dry, barren desert thirty-six thousand feet below him. The drink cart stopped at his row, and he ordered another double to reflect more.

As Dan sipped the drink, his mind flashed back to being in purgatory.

"Maddie and Machelle. Part of the probationary phase is feeling what you'll be doing to other souls and the severe understanding of the abilities that we have and hold so sacred," Ethel said matter-of-factly.

"How do you mean?" Machelle asked.

"Like some kind of gang initiation? Or hazing like in the military?" Maddie questioned.

"Kind of like how law enforcement gets pepper-sprayed or tasered before they are allowed to carry them. You must understand the severity of what we do and empathize with those who go through purgatory. It isn't fair if you can put someone through this without any understanding of how it feels. Make sense?" Ethel explained.

"I understand. How many cycles would we have to go through, though?" Machelle inquired.

"Just one, but it will be as brutal for you. Although you two don't have crimes to atone for like the others who go through this, your experiences will still deal with your biggest fears and be terrible for you. And, during it, you won't have any knowledge of all of this. It will be like you just showed up and woke up there. We can't show any mercy on you two during your phase. We all went through it."

"What was your version of purgatory?" Maddie excitably questioned.

"I had to be buried alive. It was horrible to live out my worst nightmare," Ethel said in dismay. "Are you two ready?"

They both nodded and disappeared.

CHAPTER TWELVE

Machelle woke up on a sailboat in a very foggy early morning. She was alone on the boat and tried to see through the fog to navigate, but it was too dense. She looked around for a flashlight to shine out to see if she could get someone's attention but to no avail. She assumed the boat's standard lights would be enough to alert any nearby vessel of her presence, although she was worried about the visibility of this white sailboat and white sails in the dense fog.

She continued to look for a flashlight, an air horn, or anything to call attention to her. She couldn't find anything nearby or topside. When she was about to head under to see if an emergency kit had anything she could use to alert, she was startled by the sound of white noise. She looked around in a panic to see where the sound was coming from. The sound seemed to be coming in from everywhere.

Machelle looked around franticly for the direction of the sound but couldn't land a location. She stared into virtual nothingness while seeking the sound. When she looked upward, she was completely stunned by what she saw.

The main sail was being used as a projector screen. Machelle stared in disbelief. She had just been looking all over the boat and hadn't seen any projector, cables, or anything. How was this happening?

The main sail screen began playing scenes from her life. She was frightened that such footage existed but was also pleased to see her family giving her so much love and attention. Although she loved those memories, she wasn't pleased to see her siblings fighting or her school antics on the screen. She was completely embarrassed to see her intimate moments with her ex-boyfriend play out in front of her. And she was ashamed of the video of her sneaking out to meet her ex and all the things they shouldn't have done. The screen slowed down and went back to white noise after.

Who the hell could have all of those images and videos? I know my family didn't record that. What kind of witchcraft is this? That was some good-quality footage, too. It wasn't typical home-video quality, she thought.

After the video stopped playing, the main sail returned to its normal appearance. The white noise sound slowly faded, echoing around her and the boat. She had no idea where she was. She couldn't get any bearings or even a general direction. The fog was so dense that not even a hint of sunlight could break through. Therefore, she couldn't even get a location of the sun on the horizon or a shadow cast down from the boat onto the water.

The boat began to move around, not by wind or current but by what felt like waves.

She quickly moved to the starboard side to see the direction of the waves and see if they could give her a clue of her whereabouts.

A wake from a boat? A wave from the ocean? Is this the ocean? Is it a lake?

She reached her hand into the water to smell and taste it. It was neither fresh nor salt water, but something in between. She grew even more confused when she looked down again to see no actual waves or wakes.

What the hell? How can the boat move without any waves, wake, or current? It was rocking like small waves! I have to try to communicate with someone. I have to figure this out! I can't deal with this anymore!

Machelle moved down into the belly of the sailboat to look for some sort of communication tool. A GPS, a radio, an air horn, or even some sort of light that could blink to get someone's attention.

She did a quick scan, hoping to find something and get back topside on the off chance that someone was passing by. She also hoped to alert someone of her position so she didn't get run over by a monster cargo tanker or something.

She continued a quick scan of the area to try and uncover something. Nothing. She moved back up top to do another search in a full circular perimeter check. While doing that, she held her breath as well. She had hoped to hear even a slight sound of a wake against a dock or shore or perhaps a fishing reel quickly unspooling during a cast. Nothing.

The boat started moving again, and she headed back down to do an in-depth search for something, anything.

There has to be something on this godforsaken boat! How can this boat be in operation and on the water? I thought everything had to be Coast Guard compliant. But there are no lights, no radios, no GPS tracker, no horn, and no life jackets! They have to be somewhere!

With that thought, she started tearing through everything from one side of the interior part of the boat to the other. Throughout this, the boat was rocking from side to side, but she was so focused on finding the communication devices that it didn't bother her too much.

While she was moving stuff around and slamming stuff about, she didn't hear the door close and lock behind her, sealing her inside the cabin. The boat started rocking even harder. That put her into more of a frenzy. She looked out the port holes to try and see if land or another boat was nearby. Nothing.

She continued her frantic search but still found nothing. The waves soon had the boat rocking so hard that she stopped searching and held on. With each wave, she looked out one port hole and down at the water. Then back to the other side. She couldn't do anything except hold on and try not to bounce around the inside of the cabin like a pinball.

She looked for any signs of wind or a storm but again, nothing. Her heart raced, and she began to truly panic. A big wave came in and dislodged her grip. She fell through the cabin and slammed her head on the corner of a cabinet, knocking her unconscious.

She woke up just minutes later but lying on her stomach. She looked to her left and saw the ceiling light at eye level! This brought her out of her headache and daze. She flipped on her backside and realized the port holes were in the water—the boat was completely upside down.

She crawled to the door to escape from the cabin but couldn't budge the door even a centimeter. She struggled with the door, trying to get to move a little. She was so focused on the door that she didn't register when something cracked. She thought it was the door frame and that she had gotten the door to budge a little bit.

It was, in fact, a crack in a seam, and the cabin was slowly beginning to fill with water. After a few more minutes of struggling with the door, she felt her leg getting wet and froze. Wide-eyed, she slowly turned and looked down to see the cabin filling with water.

It was then that she realized she was all alone, and nothing could help her get out of this situation. In a defeated manner, she slowly looked around, knowing there would be no tool to save her. The boat wasn't equipped, and she was doomed. She was helpless. Her worst fear was coming true. She was going to drown.

But Machelle refused to go down without a fight. She started kicking and hitting the door with everything she had within her. She frantically fought while the cabin was slowly consumed with water.

In a matter of minutes, the cabin was nearing the capacity where the water would hold back too much of her energy in her fight to escape. She continued to give it her all but saw no progress. She finally swam to the table part and held herself up with the bolted leg to the floor.

Seriously, what the hell? If there was even an adjustable wrench on this shitty-ass boat, I could have unbolted this table and used it as a battering ram. But no! Instead, I'm going to drown. Alone. No one will find me. I bet I'm in the Bermuda Triangle. I can't believe I'm about to die, and in the ONLY way that I wouldn't want to go. Why not something quick? Oh well. Almost go time anyway.

Machelle held her head up to find the last bits of air before the cabin filled with water, and she was fully encapsulated.

How do I act in these last moments? Should I sit with my legs crossed? Should I swim laps until I'm done? Do I hold on to the table leg? Do I look out the port hole? What does one do?

She decided to be comical and sit in different poses. She tried to do underwater dancing. She finally decided to finish by expelling her air and last bit of energy by swimming around. She hoped this would hurry up the process and end her agony.

Once her air was out of her lungs and her energy was gone, she had a massive anxiety attack. She didn't want to die and feared what the next minute or two held. She tried to hit the wall in a very last attempt to escape. It was like a movie slowly turning off. Everything slowly faded away, and her body began to relax. Her mind went clear, and everything ended up going black.

◇————————◇

"Do you have problems with constipation? If so, we have a solution for you." The commercial blared through the speakers.

"Our product is clinically proven to get obstructed bowels moving again. Our success rate is well above ninety-eight percent." The voice continued throughout the enclosure of the car.

Maddie sat behind the wheel, pressing the button to skip to another channel. She heard the sound of the radio quickly skipping through stations to land on one with good service.

"So, there I was on this boat outing, and I had to poop! I was in the middle of this big-ass lake! Where was I going to go? I hopped in the water to 'cool off,' took my trunks off, and pushed one out in the water. I couldn't mess up this boat outing with a new chick. It wasn't like I could say, 'Excuse me, miss, I need to go take a massive poop.' You all know what I mean?" the comedian said, getting a good laugh from the crowd.

Maddie didn't find this funny at all. She pressed the seek button to get to the next radio station. The sound clicked through stations and landed on another.

She was pleased to hear one of her favorite songs on that station. She decided to leave it. Well, until a lame song or some other commercial about shit came on.

She was thoroughly enjoying the song but not the traffic. She couldn't believe how horrible the traffic was. She tried to think how she had even gotten in the traffic to begin with but got sidetracked when she saw a state transportation vehicle drive past on the shoulder with its orange lights flashing.

How is traffic this terrible? There can't be any way they are doing scheduled road work now. Not during rush hour! If so, that's some freaking bullshit and should be illegal. Talk about impeding the flow of traffic! People have lives after work! I hope it's just an accident and things will be cleared up soon. If it is an accident, I hope everyone is okay.

Maddie forgot her song and tuned it out with her inner thoughts. The screen then went clear. In a quick panic, she tried pressing the power button on the touchscreen, but nothing transpired. She turned to the dashboard to see if she had lost all power. She still had full power in the vehicle.

Why did the screen cut out? That's really odd.

With the traffic not moving and the entertainment gone, she was a bit worried about things hurrying up. She quickly scanned traffic, the mirrors, the dashboard, and back to the screen, hoping for some magical reset by her looking away.

The screen turned back on but showed Mel in the hospital holding Maddie as a freshly swaddled newborn.

Maddie smiled and teared up, seeing this before realizing what was happening. The video continued playing through Maddie's life. It showed her walking to school and confronting the man at the coffee shop. It showed them moving and everything since and between.

Who has this much video of me? I have led a very quiet and mostly off-the-grid life. There is no freaking way that anyone has this much imagery of me. I must be dreaming because this can't even be remotely true.

The screen went black, and she felt a bubbling feeling in her lower stomach.

Must be nerves from watching that impossible video.

Her lower stomach growled and made some gurgling noises.

"Ugh! Stupid traffic! I hope we get moving soon! I don't know how much longer my nerves can hold! Stupid anxiety about sitting in traffic and then that weird-ass video. I just want to get home!" she shouted at the rear bumper in front of her.

Her stomach gurgled again, more urgently.

She squirmed in her seat, trying to get comfortable while turning on the radio again.

"Do you have problems with constipation? If so, we have a solution for you. Our product is clinically proven to get obstructed bowels moving again. Our success rate is well above ninety-eight percent," the commercial began to play again.

Her stomach began to roil, bubbling and gurgling as she squirmed uncomfortably.

Ugh! I gotta get out of this freaking nowhere traffic! I need a bathroom! she yelled in her head. *Maybe if I could get over and get to an off-ramp, I can get to a clean toilet,* she thought as she scanned to get three lanes over to her right. *Well, the toilet won't be clean when I'm done with it,* she continued with her thoughts and then an audible giggle while she turned on her blinker.

Her stomach cramped painfully, physically and audibly reminding her of the urgency.

She could get over one lane but still had two more to go to even be in a lane to exit the jam-packed freeway. She looked and squinted to see what the distant sign read.

"Ah, man! Two-and-a-half miles until the next exit? What the hell?" she yelled out.

Okay, she thought, trying to calm herself. *I'll get over two lanes, which should still give me plenty of time.*

"So, there I was on this boat outing, and I had to poop! I was in the middle of this big-ass . . ." The next radio station started to play.

Seriously? I just listened to that horrible comedian! Are there only two stations in this whole city?

Her stomach gurgled again violently.

She turned on her blinker again and tried to get over another lane. The cars in that lane kept speeding up and staying bumper to bumper, not letting her in.

"Ah, come on! Let me in!" she yelled into her car, with rolled-up windows and closed sunroof. "I have to get to a bathroom! Haven't any of you ever been in dire need of a bathroom?"

She kept her blinker on and frantically looked left to right throughout the lane, hoping for an opening. She kept at it, but the cars honked in anger every time she tried to inch in. This pissed her off even more.

Maybe this is somehow just a weird stretch of assholes that would never help another soul. Selfish douchenuggets! she thought as she tried between every car passing.

When she turned to her left and found traffic in front of her, she sat in her seat in disbelief and threw her hands to the car roof. She witnessed a car that wouldn't let her pass, stop and let another vehicle in.

Her stomach continued to churn noisily.

"Are you freaking kidding me?" she yelled in pure disbelief. One hand pressed down on her abdomen as she tried to hold back the inevitable. She continued, "I could be one lane away from the exit lane if you weren't such a douchebag and let me over. What? She has bigger tits than me?"

Maddie was shocked by her anger about the situation. Her stomach kept gurgling angrily at her while she fought through getting over two whole lanes. This continued for about a mile down the road.

A car was finally kind enough to let her into the lane to her right.

Okay, one more lane to go, and I still have a little over a mile left. Should be plenty of time.

The last mile she completely tuned out the radio and all of the poop commercials, songs, and comedy skits. She was just glad to get one lane closer to the off-ramp.

"Do you have problems with constipation?" the commercial started again.

"Ah, shut the hell up!" she yelled as she punched the power button to turn off the radio. The screen went black.

Her stomach continued its protest, the cramping growing worse.

"Do you have problems with constipation?" the commercial repeated as the screen for the sound system turned on by itself and the volume increased almost to maximum.

"Screw you!" she screamed at her car radio screen and pressed the power button again.

The screen turned back on at normal brightness and lower volume, "Do you have problems with constipation?"

"Come on! Let me over!" she pleaded as she tried inching her way over again.

Someone finally honked and gestured to let her move into the far-right lane. She waved a few times to show her gratitude.

Phew! Thank you. Thank you. Thank you! Now, I just need to get through this last bit of a half mile of traffic.

She was grateful to be around half a mile from the exit and on her way to the bathroom. She tried not to pay attention to the cramping in her roiling stomach and the sudden fullness in her bladder. She just kept telling herself that she was almost there.

Her lane moved at a decent pace for a short time, and she began feeling excitement and hope. She wondered what it could have been that was tearing her stomach apart. Maybe the bean and cheese burrito she'd had for lunch? The more she thought about food, the more her stomach gurgled in protest.

She got to a point where she could finally see the exit sign. The eighteen-wheeler sitting two vehicles in front of her blocked any view of the off-ramp and what she should expect.

The *Exit Only—This Lane* sign was now above her, and she was excited to finally get off the freeway. She continued behind the semi with glee. The ending to this torture was near!

As the semi kept trucking along, she followed, eagerly awaiting the off-ramp. She was so eager that she kept her blinker on. She saw flashing lights as she glimpsed a small break between the city walls that kept freeway noise out of the very close neighborhoods. It was a sea of orange lights mixed with red and blue.

Maybe this is it. The accident is finally on the shoulder, and we can get by. Maybe everyone shouldn't bottleneck on the freeway to stare at every accident anyway.

"Are you FREAKING kidding me?" she screamed as she saw a patrol car sitting next to a construction sign indicating that the off-ramp was closed. She screamed again as she gripped the steering wheel with both hands and shook it while her hair flailed back and forth.

"There is no way that I'll make it now! I'm going to have to throw the car in park and make a run for the guardrail," she said aloud as she tried to process it all and develop a plan.

She got a short distance down the freeway and didn't see any more signs around, so she pulled onto the shoulder. She knew she had to make a run for it.

She unbuckled her seatbelt, looked around, and went to open her door.

Her door wouldn't open. Puzzled, she struggled to open her door, but it wouldn't budge. She tried fiddling with the lock and handle but nothing. Her frustrated movements and anxieties about pooping where someone might see her made her stomach churn even more.

She finally realized that she still had the car in drive, which was why the doors wouldn't open. She put the car in park, then looked around one more time. She slowly opened her door and looked around, seeing an endless stream of cars creeping along the freeway.

She bolted and made a run for it. She ran around in front of her car and toward the guardrail. She was so fixated on finding a spot with any privacy that she didn't realize how her anxiety and fast movements just added to her churning bowels.

With a final hurdle over the railing, she couldn't hold it any longer.

Embarrassment flooded over her. She didn't turn to notice who could see the light-brown running feces running down her legs. She just stripped off her shorts and underwear and squatted behind the post of a guardrail. She faced the wall with shame and hoped nobody had witnessed what had just happened.

She finished up her bowel and bladder movements, knowing she couldn't put back on her clothes—they were totally ruined. She didn't even have anything to help her clean up. As tears streamed down her face, she shamefully turned back to the traffic. Holding her soiled garments in front of her privates, she hurried to her passenger-side door hoping to get in and limit the number of people who might see her. She couldn't get in that door, so she tried the rear passenger door. Nothing.

She realized she would have to go to the driver's side to get back into her car. She quickly moved around the side of the car, opened the driver's door, sat down, and stared straight ahead. She couldn't help but feel like eyes were on her.

She looked in the rearview mirror and the side mirrors to see the vehicles behind her. Sure enough, all the occupants were focused on her. She looked to her left to see all of the cars to her left staring at her with wide eyes. She looked at the cars in front of her and saw that the drivers were either turned around or looking at her in the mirrors.

She was so saddened that she reclined her seat all the way back and buried her face in her hands to cry. She kept her eyes closed as the tears found their way out of her closed eyelids. She wept and wept until she passed out.

◇────────────◇

The aircraft began to bump around a bit as the pilots changed altitude during the initial descent into San Diego. This startled Dan and brought him out of his flashbacks. He quickly finished his vodka tonic. He thought about hitting the San Diego International Airport terminal bar before catching his rideshare home. He tried not to process it all, but the more alcohol that hit his liver, the more he couldn't avoid it.

The plane landed, Dan deplaned, then headed straight to the bar. He ordered a double shot of whiskey, neat. He threw it back, headed to baggage claim to get his bag, and then caught a rideshare home. He avoided conversation with his rideshare driver and didn't care about the bad rating he might get for not being pleasant. After the driver's failed attempts at conversation, he turned up the music on the back speakers and made a phone call.

I wonder what this guy's karma level is. I wish I could see everyone's karma levels on the plane and in the airport, too. How crazy would it be to be able to see the pilot's karma level? Eh, kind of scary to think about. It would be cool and interesting, though.

The rideshare vehicle arrived, and the driver didn't get out to help Dan with his bag. He just popped the trunk and let his passenger get his own bag while he carried on his conversation in what sounded like an Eastern European language.

Dan closed the hatchback latch and walked to the front door with his keys. Dan was excited to see Juliet and to pass out with her willing puppy cuddles. He walked in and thanked his best friend for bringing Juliet back while Juliet slobbered all over him, excitedly whining.

The two men gave each other a quick bro hug, and Dan's friend caught a whiff of booze still clinging to Dan. "So Vegas was really fun, eh?"

"Maybe one day I could tell you about it. The show and limo rides around the Strip were phenomenal. I truly appreciate you taking care of the house and my sweet Juliet, especially on such short notice,"

Dan replied.

"I'm going to do some reading and hit the bed soon. I've got an early flight back home tomorrow."

"Definitely early bed for me too, brother. I'll see ya in the morning. If I'm not up by a certain time, wake me up. I'll still take ya to the airport," Dan said on his way to the kitchen.

Dan fed Juliet and took her out to go to the bathroom before they headed back in for an early bedtime. When Dan told her it was time for bed, she came sprinting down the hall, jumping into bed to claim her spot at the end of the bed.

Dan took another quick shot and set the glass down on the nightstand. He lay down, and Juliet settled against his legs. Dan passed out after browsing the internet and catching up on some emails.

He woke up from a crazy dream and had to pee badly. He went to the toilet, grabbing his phone off his nightstand. It was two-thirty in the morning as he stood there peeing and texting himself the details of the dream before going back to sleep. He liked to write down the details of his dreams while they were fresh in his mind, especially bizarre dreams like the one he'd just experienced.

He clicked send. Dan saw his text come through but was shocked when his keyboard began to type.

What's your decision?

He shook his head and looked at the phone again, but the message had cleared. When he woke up the next morning to check his messages and saw the message from himself, then put the phone back on the nightstand as he rubbed his eyes and stretched.

His phone vibrated with another message.

Dan picked the phone back up and looked at the screen.

Well, what's your decision???

He took a deep breath and began to type.

I'm in. What's next?

It didn't take long for the next message to come through.

Welcome to MaCoven.